The Secret of the Himala

by Hal G. Evarts

Jerry Dunham could hardly ...s luck. A team of American scientists was going to Nepal, and Jerry was a member of the expedition. Their assignment was clear-cut: to bring back the abominable snowman, the legendary yeti of the Himalayas.

Following tracks of the mysterious beast in the vast, icy wilderness, the men encountered innumerable dangers —natural and manmade. Jerry soon realized his selection for the trip was an honor and a challenge. From the start mammalogist Tom Malloy openly showed his dislike and disapproval. His antagonism toward Jerry threatened the morale of the whole group.

Then strange instances of sabotage began to occur with alarming frequency. Equipment was damaged, a man injured. Someone was out to make sure the expedition failed. Jerry was determined to uncover the identity of the mysterious saboteur and to prove to Tom Malloy that he could do a man's job—and do it well.

Each step of the harrowing search for the elusive yeti—the secret of the Himalayas — builds up suspense and tension. In this exciting tale of high adventure Hal G. Evarts' exceptional talent as a storyteller is at its best.

THE SECRET
OF THE
HIMALAYAS

THE SECRET OF THE HIMALAYAS

by Hal G. Evarts

CHARLES SCRIBNER'S SONS New York

For Ginger, Bill, and John

CHAPTER 1

IT began as a routine Monday for Jerry. With one exception there was nothing to distinguish it from any other day of the week. Zoology II lab fell on Monday afternoon and that was his favorite class. Even though he was only a freshman, and most of the others were upper-class premedical students, he looked forward to it. He liked everything about laboratory work—dissecting animals, peering through a microscope, the smell of formaldehyde.

He mounted a piece of rabbit tissue on a glass plate and began sketching its muscular system. Then somebody tapped him on the shoulder. "Dean's office wants you, Dunham," the professor said. "Right away."

3

"The dean?" Jerry blinked up at him. "Dean who?"

"Dean of Men. What have you been up to?"

Jerry grinned but his throat felt tight. A summons from the Dean of Men did sound ominous, though he couldn't imagine what he might have done. An emergency, he thought. His family? Something about his scholarship? His grades? Surely it meant some kind of trouble. Hurriedly he gathered his notes, stowed his equipment in his locker, and left the lab.

Because it housed a collection of mammal skeletons, the Zoology Department was known on campus as "The Menagerie." Jerry caught a glimpse of his reflection as he passed the saber-tooth tiger case in the corridor. He looked scared. He was scared, he admitted. In seven months at State U. he'd never been inside the dean's office. It was all he could do not to break into a run across Memorial Court and up the stairs.

A secretary asked him to wait and he took a chair and tried not to watch the hands of the electric clock. Somewhere a typewriter clacked and voices buzzed faintly behind the pebbled glass of an inner-office door. Presently a senior, a zoology major whom he knew slightly, stepped out. They stared at each other in mutual surprise, then the secretary motioned Jerry forward.

"Come in, Dunham," the dean said. "I imagine that you're wondering what this is all about."

"Yes, sir," Jerry stammered.

"Don't look so worried." The dean smiled. "I won't bite." He led the way through a second door into another office, where an elderly white-haired man sat behind a mahogany desk studying some papers spread out before him. "Here's the last on your list, Mr. Trevor," the dean said in a respectful tone. "Dunham, this is Mr. Gordon Lindsay Trevor. Now I'll leave you two alone."

As the door clicked shut behind him, Jerry felt his throat go dry again, in spite of the dean's reassurance. Gordon Lindsay Trevor was a name you read in the newspapers. Banker. Philanthropist. Chairman of the board. University trustee. There must be some mistake, he decided. They had him mixed up with some other Dunham.

For a long minute Mr. Trevor peered at him from under fierce bushy eyebrows. Then he barked, "How old are you?"

"Nineteen, sir."

"Humph! That's pretty young for what we have in mind. But you look fairly husky. Ever done any mountain climbing?"

"A little. I was raised in the Rockies. And I worked for the Forest Service the last two summers."

"Aren't you behind your class?"

"Yes, sir. I stayed out a year after high school to earn money for college. I got a part-time job in the Natural History Museum."

"I see." Mr. Trevor referred to one of the papers on his desk. "It says here you won a scholarship for academic excellence. But I like to size up a man face to face. Tell me this, Mr. Dunham—" His keen blue eyes swung back to Jerry. "Tell me, why did you choose State University, instead of some other? Take your time. Think about it."

"That's easy, Mr. Trevor. I came here because they have one of the best zoology faculties in the country."

"Is that what you want to be, a professor?"

"No, sir. A naturalist."

"You seem to know your own mind." Mr. Trevor came to his feet, crossed the room, and stood peering out the window at the hurrying crowds of students in the bright sunshine below. When he turned his expression had softened. "I had a grandson about your age. He attended this university as I did many years ago. He wanted to be a naturalist, too."

"Did he change *his* mind?"

"No. No, he didn't." Mr. Trevor sighed, and his manner became brusque once more. "Some weeks ago you filed an application for a field research project. Do you recall that?"

He did remember. At the beginning of the spring semester a notice had been tacked to the bulletin board in the lab. It was an announcement to the effect that one undergraduate from the School of Natural Sciences would be chosen to take part in an expedition being organized to survey the flora and fauna of an unnamed foreign area. Any interested male student in good standing could enter the competition. Jerry had filled out a long, complicated questionnaire even though he'd known he didn't stand much chance.

"We've narrowed the applicants down to half a dozen," Mr. Trevor went on. "You have a good record, but ordinarily we wouldn't consider a freshman, so don't pin your hopes too high."

Jerry swallowed. "Is that why you sent for me?"

"We weigh a number of things about each boy. His class-work first, of course; his overall experience, personality, his ability to work with other people, his know-how in the out-doors. The one who wins is going to be a member of a highly expert team, so we have to be sure to pick the very best."

"Where is the expedition going?"

"I'll answer that question by asking you another. Is there any reason, personal or family or health, why you couldn't leave on short notice to be gone for as long as six months?"

"Six months! But what about my classes?"

"Young man," Mr. Trevor said dryly, "the lecture hall is not the whole of education. If this opportunity should come your way, I advise you not to miss it. I'd give anything to go myself."

"No, sir. What I meant," Jerry hastened to explain, "it's sort of sudden and I don't have much money."

"Money won't be any problem."

"Then I'd be ready to leave anytime. Tomorrow! Right now!"

Mr. Trevor chuckled. "I believe you would at that." He then proceeded to fire a barrage of questions at Jerry. How long had he been an Explorer Scout? Was he subject to altitude sickness? How much had he camped in the open? Had he ever collected and prepared specimens in the field? By the time he finished Jerry's head was spinning. For a long while afterward Mr. Trevor was silent as he gazed out the window again, as if he were looking at some object far away. "I wish—" he began.

"Sir?" Jerry said.

"Never mind. Just an old man dreaming out loud." With a faint smile he thrust out his hand. The interview was over. "We'll let you know. Good afternoon."

Jerry thanked him and walked back across the campus in a

daze. What connection a man like Gordon Lindsay Trevor had with a scientific expedition he couldn't understand. When you came right down to it, Mr. Trevor had been careful not to reveal much solid information. His hint about mountains could point to almost any place, and the clue about being gone six months didn't tell much either. Wherever it was, Jerry realized that his chances were still mighty slim. One out of six. Sixteen and two-thirds per cent. He couldn't afford to dream like Mr. Trevor. He had two hours of missed lab-work to make up.

His evening job was washing dishes in the Student Union, and afterwards he did his homework in the library, but his mind kept wandering to distant places. Africa had high mountains. That could be the expedition's destination. Maybe South America, the Andes. Or New Guinea in the South Pacific. He got out an atlas and pored over the maps. When he returned to the dormitory his roommate was getting ready for bed.

"I hear the dean called you on the carpet, Jerry," he said. "Don't tell me you're flunking out."

Jerry laughed. He was bursting to tell somebody, but he knew very little really. "It wasn't anything," he said. "False alarm."

That night he found it hard to sleep, tossing and turning as he puzzled over the reason for Mr. Trevor's secrecy, but finally he drifted off. He dreamed he was chasing some two-headed animal up an icy peak with a butterfly net.

Next morning was the same. He attended classes and listened dutifully, but couldn't seem to concentrate. He went through the day in a sort of trance, knowing all the while how foolish this was. Mr. Trevor had warned him not to count his chickens. But a picture kept floating before his eyes—a tantalizing picture of a camp set high against some vast snowy range. He checked out books on natural history expeditions, most of which he'd read before, and studied over them again. But as the days passed and no word came, his last dim hope faded.

Saturdays he had a job in an off-campus taxidermy shop. It didn't pay much, but he felt at home among the stuffed heads and furs and animal skins. The work was practical, good basic training for a future naturalist. The only way to forget his disappointment, he told himself, was by keeping busy.

About twelve o'clock, when his employer was out to lunch, a rangy, weathered man with a pipe between his teeth stepped into the shop. The stranger took his time looking around, as if he'd never hurried in his life. "Would you be Dunham?" he asked.

"That's right," Jerry told him.

"I'm Sebold," he said. "Dr. Carl Sebold."

Suddenly Jerry's heart started to thump. If he had been awed in the presence of Mr. Trevor, he was practically tongue-tied now. Carl Sebold was an international authority and curator of mammals at the top museum in the country. Jerry had read all his books and the accounts of expeditions he had led. But he wasn't going to let his hopes go soaring again, not this time. "Can I help you, Dr. Sebold?" he managed to say.

"I think so," Dr. Sebold said. "Your roommate told me I'd probably find you here."

"You—you're looking for me?"

"If your name's Jerry Dunham I am." Dr. Sebold smiled. "How about a bite of lunch?"

A minute ago he had been hungry, thinking of his sandwiches in the back room. But now he'd lost his appetite. He knew he couldn't swallow a mouthful. "I can't leave now. Some customers might come in."

"Then we'll talk here." Dr. Sebold walked over to a mounted deer head and examined it deliberately. "Is this some of your work?"

"Yes, sir."

"Very realistic. My own staff couldn't do better." Dr. Sebold moved on from one specimen to another, peering and poking, completely absorbed, while Jerry watched in an agony of impatience. Presently he finished, tamped more tobacco into his pipe, and puffed out a cloud of blue smoke. When he had it drawing to his satisfaction he looked up and said, "You're a fortunate young man."

Jerry could only nod.

"Mr. Trevor is a great believer in youth. Especially today, when the United States is competing with foreign countries in education and science and research. He feels we should give our young people the best training available. You made quite an impression on him."

"I did?"

"He had a grandson," Dr. Sebold continued. "A promising student in natural history, who died in a tragic accident last year. Ever since, Mr. Trevor has been anxious to organize and finance a field expedition in the boy's memory. He has asked me to lead it. And he has chosen you to go along as observer and, well—a junior member."

Jerry let out a whoop. He couldn't help himself. He wanted to pound Dr. Sebold on the back and do a jig. He'd made it! Then he grinned sheepishly. "I'm sorry. I wasn't thinking how Mr. Trevor must feel about his grandson. I guess I'm sort of excited."

"Who wouldn't be." Dr. Sebold laughed and put out his hand. "Congratulations, Jerry. Welcome to the team."

And then he grew serious. A major expedition, he explained, cost hundreds of thousands of dollars; it wasn't any vacation trip. The members were all years older than Jerry, specialists with advanced degrees, dedicated men who hoped to expand human knowledge by their findings. Many qualified scientists eager to go had been turned down. Including a college student on such an expedition was an experiment, and Jerry should feel honored.

"I do, Dr. Sebold," he said soberly. "I'll work hard, I promise you."

"I'm sure you will, Jerry. I'll admit I had my doubts when Mr. Trevor first suggested this. But after meeting you, I'm sold."

"Will I be the only student?"

"The only one," Dr. Sebold said. "So I want you to be prepared in case there's any talk or criticism. Sometimes people oppose new ideas. Just remember that you won this on your own, and you have every right to be proud."

"How soon are—is the expedition leaving?" He couldn't

bring himself to say "we." He didn't feel that he belonged yet. He was still an outsider, a pea-green freshman with a lucky horseshoe.

"In about two weeks. We have a lot to do." Dr. Sebold glanced at his watch and swung abruptly toward the door. "I have an appointment with Mr. Trevor now, but we'll get together tonight and talk some more."

"Tonight? But—but—" Dr. Sebold was nearly through the doorway. "Where are you going?"

"Oh. Did I forget to mention that?" Dr. Sebold gave him an absent-minded glance. "For various reasons we want as little newspaper publicity as possible. That's why there hasn't been an official announcement. We're going to Nepal."

"Nepal?"

"The Himalayas. Near Mount Everest." Observing Jerry's startled look, Dr. Sebold broke into another laugh. "See you in Katmandu," he said.

Through the window Jerry watched his long figure disappear into a car. He felt as if he could scarcely breathe. "Did you hear that?" he said aloud to the deer head on the wall. He rolled the phrase over on his tongue. It had a fine resounding ring. " 'See you in Katmandu.' "

Katmandu, he learned from a reference volume in the bookcase, was the capital of a small Asian kingdom squeezed between India and Tibet. The lowland jungles abounded in tigers, elephants, rhinos, and other big game. The northern frontier, the mighty Himalayan Range, claimed the highest peaks on earth. Animals were to be found there as well, some at great elevations—snow leopards, bears, ibex, musk deer and tahr. Much of the region was still unexplored. It sounded like a naturalist's paradise.

The next few days were the busiest he had ever known. That evening Dr. Sebold outlined their plans. Members of the expedition were to assemble in New York. They would complete their final outfitting there and fly together across the Atlantic and on to India. The heavy equipment and supplies already had been shipped ahead by steamer. All Jerry had to do was get himself ready.

On Sunday Dr. Sebold drove him home to help break the news to his parents. His mother hugged him and wiped her eyes and worried about his clothes. His father gave his shoulder an extra hard squeeze and slipped a ten dollar bill in his pocket. It reminded him a little of the first time he had gone off to summer camp alone. Only Nepal was halfway around the world.

"I know this is very sudden," Dr. Sebold told his mother and father, "and it breaks into Jerry's school year. I'll be frank with you, Mr. and Mrs. Dunham. We've had to advance the departure date of our expedition."

"Why?" Mr. Dunham asked.

"As you know, the Chinese Communists have seized Tibet. Their troops are stationed along the border. For the past few years the Nepalese government has encouraged scientific expeditions like ours. But the Communists have ways of bringing pressure on small neighboring countries. It's barely possible that they might be able to persuade the Nepalese to cancel our entry permit. So we're anxious to get there before anything like that happens."

14

"Is it dangerous?" Jerry's mother said.

"Not in my own opinion. The Nepalese are wonderful people, friendly to Americans and anti-Communist. But I want to lay all my cards on the table before you give Jerry your final permission."

His father and mother exchanged a long look. Jerry held his breath. Then Mr. Dunham nodded. "We know what kind of a boy Jerry is, Dr. Sebold," he said. "If there should be trouble, we have every confidence he can take care of himself."

Dr. Sebold smiled. "I don't know him as well as you do. But I'm inclined to agree. One thing I am sure of though: neither of you will ever regret this."

Back at campus on Monday, he got permission from the dean to take a leave of absence. On his return in the fall he would have make-up exams. He applied for a passport, had his medical shots, and bought the boots and special alpine clothes he would need for living in high altitudes weeks at a time. There seemed to be a thousand last-minute details that he would never finish, as the days raced past. Then *the* day dawned, and he was packed and ready, all his goodbyes said.

Dr. Sebold had returned to New York to direct the expedition's final preparations. Only Mr. Trevor saw him off at the airport. As they waited by the loading gate, Jerry fumbled for words. "Mr. Trevor, I don't know how to say it—"

"Then don't," Mr. Trevor said gruffly. "This is my pleasure too, you know."

"All the same I'm grateful for everything you've done."

Mr. Trevor snorted and blew his nose and looked away.

"There's one thing you haven't been told yet: the primary purpose of this expedition. Maybe you've guessed."

"What's that, Mr. Trevor?"

"Many scientists and the public pooh-pooh the whole idea. That's why we've tried to keep this quiet. It's to prove whether a creature such as the yeti does, or does not actually exist."

"Yeti?"

"Better known as the abominable snowman."

Jerry was too astounded to answer. Just then the gate swung open and passengers surged forward. Mr. Trevor gave him a brief farewell handshake. "Good hunting, son."

A minute later he stumbled up the platform into the plane and found a seat. He peered out the window but Mr. Trevor had vanished. Then he became aware that a stewardess was beside him, asking his destination. He had to resist an impulse to tell her he was bound for Mount Everest to catch an abominable snowman. He wondered if she would believe him. He hardly believed it himself.

CHAPTER 2

THE Manhattan skyline loomed against the evening sky as Jerry rode into New York City. The airport limousine deposited him in front of the hotel where he'd been told to report, and he asked for Dr. Sebold's room number. An elevator shot him to the twentieth floor and he hurried along the corridor. Soon he would be meeting the other members of the expedition, the men with whom he was to live and work for months to come, and it was important to start off on the right foot.

The door was slightly ajar and he paused to straighten his tie. A voice came to him from inside the room. "Ridiculous," a man was declaring loudly. "A schoolboy! We have enough problems without playing baby sitter, Carl."

"Calm down, Tom," Dr. Sebold's voice answered. "Dunham is no schoolboy. Give him a chance."

Jerry's upraised arm froze but his face felt fiery. They were talking about him.

"Old man Trevor must be balmy," the speaker called Tom said. "Because he's a multi-millionaire he thinks he can saddle us with some teen-ager."

"I'll admit it's unusual," Dr. Sebold said, "but without Mr. Trevor there wouldn't be an expedition. He put up the funds and it's his privilege to send whomever he wants, whether you approve or not."

"I don't care if this Dunham is a bright kid. He's still a kid and he'll be a nuisance, always underfoot. Don't expect me to look after him."

Rooted to the floor, Jerry wished he could bolt back to the elevator and escape, but his feet wouldn't move. And then he grew angry. Angry at a man who condemned people sight unseen. He knocked firmly and waited until the door swung open. "Here he is now," Dr. Sebold exclaimed, apparently unaware that Jerry had overheard. "How are you? Have a good flight?"

"Fine, thanks." Jerry walked in and stared at the wedge-shouldered red-haired man standing by the window.

"Jerry, this is Dr. Tom Malloy, mammalogist from Eastern University. My second in command."

Tom Malloy nodded but didn't offer to shake hands. He was in his early thirties, Jerry guessed, and his pale blue eyes were coolly distant.

"Tom is quite a mountain climber," Dr. Sebold said. "He's

made two Himalayan trips already. We're lucky to have him with us. You'll work directly under him, Jerry."

He tried to sound enthusiastic. "That's great. I've heard about your work, Dr. Malloy."

Malloy shrugged. "We're bunking together tonight. Come on, I'll show you."

Jerry followed his broad back down the hall into another room where Malloy's belongings were strewn over the furniture. Obviously annoyed, Malloy cleared off one bed while Jerry unpacked his flight bag. Making an effort at conversation, he said, "What chance do you think we have of finding a snowman?"

"Have you read the literature on the subject?"

"Some of it."

"Then you should know it's mostly nonsense. Footprints in the snow. Mysterious noises in the night. Old wives' tales by superstitious natives. No white man has ever seen one. If you ask me, it's a wild goose chase."

Jerry looked up at him with curiosity. "If you don't believe in them," he said, "why are you going on the expedition?"

Malloy reddened. "I'm in a bad mood today. Here, I'll show you something." He fished in a suitcase, drew out some object, and unrolled it on the bed. It looked like a piece of animal fur about six inches square, reddish brown in color.

"I got this two summers ago from Sangpur Lamasery on the Nepal border," Malloy said. "The monks swore it's part of a yeti that had been trapped. I had to pay a fortune for it. Sebold tells me you've done some taxidermy. What do you make of it?"

Jerry ran his fingers over the pelt. The hairs were stiff, almost like bristles, and set close together. The dry, scaly skin had the musty odor of great age, although it was remarkably well preserved. "It might be some species of bear," he said cautiously. "But I've never seen anything like it."

"Neither has anybody else. I've had experts run it through every test in the book, and nobody can identify it." Malloy's eyes lit up. "That's why I'm going back. Not for any non-existent snowman. But to find this animal."

"How old is this specimen supposed to be?" Jerry asked.

"The lamas said at least two hundred years. My bearers thought closer to three. But time means nothing over there."

"Then the species could be extinct by now?"

"Who knows?" Malloy said. "I have to run some errands now. See you later."

Left alone in the room, Jerry studied the hide more thoroughly under a magnifying glass and laid it back on top of Malloy's suitcase. If the best mammalogists in America couldn't guess at its origin, how could he? Yeti? Himalayan bear? Some strange beast unknown to science? Or a creature that had died out centuries ago? Whatever it might be, he felt a ripple of excitement. Somewhere at some time such an animal had existed. It was not just another myth like the unicorn or the sea monster. This scrap of skin and fur was real. And Tom Malloy, for all his scoffing, believed in it, too.

Next morning he met two other members: Dr. Fred Snodgrass, the ornithologist, and Ross Howe, the anthropologist, a round short man who looked as if he couldn't climb a ladder without panting. It turned out, however, that Howe was a

Himalayan veteran, with climbs on Annapurna and Makalu
to his credit, while Snodgrass had done all the major North
American peaks. They were friendly and helpful, offering
Jerry advice. Except for Malloy, he felt he had been accepted
as part of the team.

During the next two days he learned how much skillful
organization went into an expedition. In addition to his own
speciality, each man was expert in at least one other field.
Ross Howe, for instance, was also a first-rate photographer.
The three other members, already in Katmandu, included a
botanist, a biologist, and a doctor. All were experienced moun-
taineers. "In a way," Dr. Sebold explained, "we're like a compact military unit. Each man has two or three jobs. We're the
general staff and shock troops, too."

"How does it work?" Jerry wanted to know.

"Well, I'm in charge of plans and personnel," Dr. Sebold
said. "Tom Malloy is logistics. That means supply and trans-
portation—in other words, when do we eat? Snodgrass is
responsible for communication; he's a radio bug. Ross Howe
is finance officer and paymaster."

"What's my job?"

Dr. Sebold handed him a large leather notebook. "You're
the official historian, Jerry. You're to keep a record of dates
and places, everything the expedition does, every specimen
we bring in. It's vital we have a complete and accurate account."

"Is there any news from our people in Nepal?" Howe asked.

"Yes, I received a cablegram this morning. So one last word
of caution. Nobody is to discuss the expedition with outsiders,

here or overseas. The political situation is tricky." Dr. Sebold looked around the table. "Any further questions, gentlemen? Conference adjourned."

The final forty-eight hours before take-off proved to be hectic. There were meetings to attend, documents to sign, last-minute supplies to check. The phone rang constantly with calls from fellow scientists wishing the expedition well, from reporters seeking a news story, but no problem seemed to fluster Dr. Sebold. Jerry marveled at the patient calm with which he stood up under such pressure. Then, an hour before departure a crisis arose.

Cramming his clothes into a bag, Malloy said to Jerry, "Where's that yeti skin I showed you the other night?"

"I put it back on top of your suitcase," Jerry told him.

"It's not there now. I haven't seen it since."

"Maybe the chambermaid moved it," Jerry suggested. "Let's look."

They searched the room hurriedly and then the closets and bathroom, looking in drawers and under furniture, but found no trace. "Are you sure?" Malloy demanded. "That's valuable, you know."

Jerry wanted to say, *Then why don't you take better care of it?* Instead he went on hunting. He was positive he had left the skin where he said, and he'd been asleep when Malloy returned later that night. Next morning it was not in sight, so he assumed that his roommate had packed it away again.

"Look here," Malloy said, "why didn't you put that back where it belonged when you were through?"

"I'm sorry, Dr. Malloy. I didn't like to open up your personal suitcase."

"Sorry!" Malloy's pink face darkened. "That's worse than careless, Dunham. You haven't been with us a week, but you've already managed to mislay an irreplaceable specimen. The only real evidence we have."

Sick and miserable, Jerry stared at him.

At that moment Dr. Sebold poked his head in the door to ask if they were almost ready. When he saw Jerry's expression he said, "Anything wrong?"

"Nothing much," Malloy said in a sarcastic tone. "Dunham's lost our yeti skin."

Dr. Sebold listened to the details and joined the search. Hastily Jerry dug through his own bag, to make certain he had not packed it there by some mistake. But as the minutes ticked away his anxiety grew. "Maybe Howe or Snodgrass borrowed it," Dr. Sebold said. "Go ask them, Jerry, will you please."

He sped down the hall, but neither man had seen the skin. When he returned to the room the hotel manager and an upset chambermaid were there, summoned by Malloy. The woman denied touching anything that looked like reddish fur. The manager promised to question his staff and send the skin on by air express if it turned up. Dr. Sebold finally got them out the door and looked at his watch. "We can't spare any more time, Tom," he said. "I don't see how, but it must be gone."

"Could someone have stolen it?" Jerry ventured.

Malloy turned on him angrily. "Don't be silly. Who would

steal a thing like that? It probably got thrown out with the dirty towels or the trash." His look of disgust said the rest. *And you're responsible, Dunham. You goofed. Don't try to pin the blame on somebody else.*

"These things happen. It was an accident, Jerry." Dr. Sebold patted him on the shoulder. "Forget it now."

Jerry couldn't forget. He knew he was in the right, but he felt under a cloud of doubt. The mystery of the yeti skin baffled him. In the weeks ahead he was to wonder more and more about its disappearance.

In the rush of getting off, however, he put the matter from his mind. By noon they were airborne and winging eastward across the Atlantic in a jet. The flight itself was uneventful. Booked straight through from London to Bombay, they made only three brief fuel halts. For all he saw, he might have been flying over his home state instead of Europe and the Middle East. By the time they nosed down to the Indian city and cleared through customs, he was so tired he wanted to sleep for a week.

But he awoke next morning in his hotel room revived and eager to go. A Hindu servant brought him tea, and while he was dressing someone tapped on the door. His visitor was a dark-skinned young man not much older than Jerry, stockily built, in a suit of tropical whites. "My name is Rishkesh Dawa," he introduced himself. "Rick for short. Welcome to Bombay."

Jerry said politely, "Good morning. Are you the hotel manager?"

When Rishkesh Dawa laughed his whole face wrinkled up

like a relief map. "I'm the expedition interpreter. Dr. Sebold asked me to look in on you."

"Then you're going with us?" Jerry said.

"Sure I am. You'll need somebody who talks yeti talk. I'm the only living expert."

Jerry grinned. "Let's hear a sample."

"Not before breakfast." Rick burst into another peal of laughter. "Come along. We'll eat first, then I'll show you the sights. Get the kinks out of your brain."

Rick rented a two-wheeled buggy he called a *ghari*, and for several hours they rode around the streets of Bombay behind a horse. He was an amusing and well-informed guide, explaining Hindu and Moslem customs, describing the architecture, and pointing out historical landmarks. By the time they returned to the hotel Jerry felt he had made a friend. Rick Dawa, the son of a prosperous Katmandu rice dealer, had been sent abroad to private school and for three years to a U.S. university, where he'd learned English. Besides his native tongue he spoke the Sherpa dialect of northeastern Nepal, which made him valuable to any expedition.

"This will be my second," he said. "I went two years ago to Sangpur Glacier."

"Then you must have gone with Tom Malloy?"

"Yes, Malloy was there," Rick said and changed the subject. "I love to climb mountains. But someday I must settle down in the family rice business."

"I thought you were a scientist," Jerry said.

"Not me. I'm just an amateur bird watcher."

Full of questions, Jerry asked the one uppermost in his

mind. "You've been there, Rick. What's your theory about yetis? Do you believe in them?"

"Believe?" Rick's black eyes squinted thoughtfully. "Yes, no, and then—maybe. I have seen footprints. Prints of something."

"If there are prints, there must be proof they exist."

"I am not sure I want to find proof, Jerry. In this crazy world of ours today, where men explore the universe, perhaps it is better to leave one little mystery unsolved. Like the child who wants to believe in Santa Claus."

Jerry smiled, for he could understand that. As a small boy he had believed for years that a mysterious animal he called the gollywhump lived in hiding under the house. When he learned it was only one of his father's tall tales, his disillusion had been painful.

"People ask me many questions," Rick went on. " 'Is the yeti human?' 'The missing link?' 'Is it an ape?' 'Do its feet point backwards?' 'Does it live to be two hundred years old?' Such legends, you have no idea! Fantastic!"

"And what do you tell them?"

"I do not laugh at them. Maybe they are right. Who can say for sure they are wrong? Anything is possible. You see, I do not have the proper scientific attitude."

"You have an open mind," Jerry said. "That's what counts."

As they passed the desk in the lobby a clerk called to Jerry and handed him a message from Dr. Sebold. He and Rick were to meet him at the Gandhi Memorial Hospital at once. All the clerk could tell them was that one of the *sahibs* had taken ill. Thoroughly alarmed, they rushed out and hailed a taxi.

Three grave men—Dr. Sebold, Tom Malloy, and Ross Howe—were pacing the floor of a hospital waiting room. In a hushed voice Dr. Sebold explained the situation. After breakfast Fred Snodgrass had been stricken with stomach cramps, which he blamed on food poisoning, but the hotel doctor had diagnosed acute appendicitis and ordered him to the hospital for an emergency operation. He was in surgery now.

They waited in an agony of suspense until a white-gowned doctor entered the room. He talked for some while to Dr. Sebold, shaking his head, and went out again. Dr. Sebold was pale under his tan as he turned to the others. "Snodgrass is out of danger, thank heaven," he said. "But what rotten luck for the poor fellow."

"How bad is it, Carl?"

"Ruptured appendix, with complications. He'll be recuperating for several weeks. Not a chance he can join us later."

The news struck them like a blow. No one had been more popular than the quiet, soft-spoken ornithologist. The expedition had lost more than his scientific skills. "Can we get a replacement?" Howe asked.

"Too late," Dr. Sebold said. "It's not humanly possible for a man to make all the arrangements and fly out here in time, even if the Nepalese government authorized a last-minute change."

"This leaves us awfully short-handed," Malloy pointed out.

"It does. But fortunately—" Dr. Sebold smiled faintly. "We have some capable substitutes. Rick—"

Rick Dawa raised a startled face. "Me?"

"As of now you're the expedition ornithologist," Dr. Sebold said. "Jerry, I seem to remember you had some experience with radio."

"Not much," Jerry told him. "I handled the walkie-talkie in the Forest Service when we were on fire patrol."

"Good enough. The communication job falls on you." Dr. Sebold looked at the others. "I don't have to tell you that losing Fred Snodgrass is a tough break for all of us. We'll have to double up and work that much harder. If you have any suggestions or gripes, now is the time to sound off. Ross? Tom?" He glanced at Malloy. "How about you?"

Malloy lifted one shoulder as if to say they had no choice.

"That's settled then. We'll take off for Katmandu tomorrow on schedule."

CHAPTER 3

Two members of the expedition advance party met them at the Katmandu airport. Dr. Harold Baimbridge, the physician, and hulking red-faced Lars Johansen, the botanist. A third member had gone ahead into the mountains to scout for a base campsite. Both men were shocked by the news of Fred Snodgrass, but they agreed it was out of the question to postpone their departure date. Even now it would be a race against winter if they hoped to cover the search area with any thoroughness.

Jerry craned his neck and peered to the north, hoping for a glimpse of the Himalayas, but heat haze obscured the view. From the windows of their plane he had looked down on tiny villages tucked among incredibly green jungle-clad hills. Here in this low, humid valley it seemed impossible that he was only a hundred miles from the world's tallest peaks.

The capital city of Nepal was a blend of East and West, of old and new. Ancient temples and shrines stood among palaces and modern stores. Mule caravans plodded through the bazaars, while vehicles of all kinds, jeeps and trucks and late model cars, raced through the narrow streets. Watching the traffic whiz by, Jerry said to his companion, "Whew, I'd hate to be a cop here!"

Rick laughed. "Ten years ago the only car in Katmandu was the royal limousine. No foreigners were allowed to enter the country. Then we had a revolution and everything changed. Now we are trying to catch up with the outside world overnight."

"Are many Americans here?"

"A few," Rick explained. "Your government sent specialists to help us. Engineers to build roads and dams, soil experts to stop erosion and improve our farms. Americans are well liked in Nepal."

"What about the Chinese?" Jerry said.

"Yes, they come too. After all, we are neighbors now. But we are not friendly neighbors. There has been trouble with their soldiers along the frontier."

The party drove to a government rest house, which was to be expedition headquarters, and the four recent arrivals went to their rooms for a much-needed sleep after the long journey. From New York they had traveled some ten thousand miles. But Jerry was too keyed up to rest. Knowing how much work lay ahead, he realized he might not have another chance to explore this exotic city in the heart of Asia.

He slipped out the door and wandered along a main thoroughfare, then turned off into a maze of back streets. The novelty of being on his own gave the strange new sights and sounds and smells a special appeal. He peered into dim lantern-lit shops and stared at the passing crowds. There were Ghurka troopers with long knives at their belts, tribesmen down from the hills, Buddhist monks in yellow robes, even a few Tibetan traders in cone-shaped hats and sheepskin cloaks.

After a while he had the feeling that he was being followed. He could not explain how he knew, nor imagine why anyone should be that curious about him, but his natural woodsman's instinct made him turn abruptly. A short, dark-skinned native in nondescript clothes stepped up with a little salaam and said, "Pardon, *sahib*. You are American, no?"

"Yes, I'm an American."

"Forgive a humble man, *sahib*. You go with countrymen to seek yeti, is it not?"

Puzzled, Jerry said carefully, "I'm with an American expedition. How did you know?"

The stranger gave him an apologetic smile, which revealed a gold front tooth. "I am Sherpa. Very first-class mountain bearer." With a flourish he presented Jerry a business card that identified him as Ang Nuri from the kingdom of Sikkim, a high-altitude bearer who had taken part in many Himalayan climbing expeditions. Excellent references, the card added, could be supplied upon request. Jerry read it over and looked at Ang Nuri with new interest.

The Sherpas, he knew, were a hardy people who lived in high valleys under the Himalayas. They were superb mountain climbers and every expedition depended on them to carry supplies up to great altitudes. Of the first two conquerors of Everest, one had been a Sherpa, and no major peak had been scaled without the aid of Sherpa porters. "Are you an Everest Tiger?"

Ang Nuri thumped his chest. "Me, Tiger. You need Tiger to climb mountain with you, yes?"

"You mean you want a job?" Jerry said.

"Ang Nuri want job to climb with Americans. Find many yeti."

"What makes you think we're looking for yetis?"

When the Sherpa laughed his gold tooth flashed in the sun. "You give me job, yes?"

Jerry shook his head. "All our men were hired weeks ago. I'm sorry, Mr. Nuri."

"Oh, too bad. Maybe somebody get sick."

"I doubt it," Jerry said. "But I'm not the boss anyway. You'll have to ask Dr. Sebold."

"Million thanks, young *sahib*. See you byenby, I think so." Ang Nuri touched a hand to his forehead, turned, and melted into the crowd. Jerry stared after him, wondering why the Sherpa had sought him out on the street if he really did want to sign on with the expedition. He had the uncomfortable feeling that Ang Nuri had been more interested in fishing for information.

When he mentioned the incident to Dr. Sebold next morning, the director frowned. "I suppose the bazaar is buzzing with gossip about us. It's no secret where we're going. Ever heard of the fellow, Rick?"

"No, he's not from these parts," Rick said. "But every Sherpa who's ever climbed a mountain calls himself an Everest Tiger so that doesn't mean much."

"If he's any good," Dr. Sebold said, "he can land a job easily. Two other parties, one Swiss and one English, are hiring all the men they can find."

"Come on, Jerry," Rick said. "I'll introduce you to a real Everest Tiger."

They walked to a large building nearby, which served as the expedition's temporary warehouse and quarters for the bearers. In the courtyard dozens of Nepalis were busy cooking breakfast over open fires, and many called greetings to Rick and grinned as he passed through to the doorway. Inside they met a squat barrel-chested little man named Kamin. Rick and Kamin spoke in the Sherpa tongue and the latter eyed Jerry curiously.

Rick broke into a laugh. "Kamin says," he translated, "that with those long legs you should be able to run up Chomolungma. That's the local name for Everest."

"But *his* legs are so short!" Jerry exclaimed. "Is he really a top climber?"

"The very top. Along with Tenzing and a few others. He's carried loads to twenty-six thousand feet. In this country, my lad, that makes him a national hero."

Kamin, Rick explained, was the *sirdar*, or head man in charge of their bearers, which included some three hundred Nepalis and eight Sherpas. This army was needed to transport the expedition's seven tons of equipment and supplies to base camp in the mountains, where no road had ever penetrated, and trails were too narrow and steep for the average pack animal. In much of Nepal man himself was the beast of burden. The Nepalis, lowland dwellers, portered up to sixteen thousand feet and occasionally higher, but above that level the high-altitude Sherpas took over. The world of eternal snow and ice was their domain.

"They've adapted to their environment," Rick said. "Look at Kamin. He has tremendous lungs for breathing that thin air. His thigh and calf muscles are tough as wire. He can sleep in snow with one blanket where you and I would freeze."

"He must hate it down in this hot climate."

"They all do," Rick said. "Kamin can hardly wait to leave."

On meeting the other Sherpas, Jerry noticed how much they resembled Kamin in build. All were short and stocky and thick-chested, with long arms and deeply weathered faces. They kept together, apart from the more numerous Nepalis, an island of quiet in the chattering throng. Even their names—Dorje, Tandu, Gylgen, Nyma, Mingma—had to his ears a remote and faraway sound.

His main job now, as Tom Malloy's assistant, was to help sort out the mountain of equipment and break it down into individual loads weighing no more than fifty pounds. This was the pack each bearer was to carry on his back. They had no packboards with shoulder straps such as he had known back home. Some men used wicker baskets, others made slings of ropes with a leather forehead band, thus leaving their arms greater freedom for balance. And most, he was astounded to see, wore no shoes nor even sandals. They preferred to climb barefooted, even on snow and ice.

He checked over the walkie-talkie radios and the short-wave receiver, on which they would depend for daily long-range weather forecasts. These and other delicate instruments, such as thermometers and barometers, had to be packed with particular care, for once they left Katmandu there would be no way to replace broken parts. Tents, sleeping bags, primus stoves, collecting jars, snow goggles—the list seemed endless. Nothing had been overlooked that might contribute to the expedition's success.

Malloy did not mention the missing yeti skin again. Presumably no trace of it had been found in New York. Jerry hoped the incident was closed, if not forgotten. And while Malloy never went out of his way to be friendly, Jerry had to admit he might have misjudged the man. It was impossible not to admire anyone so absorbed in his job.

Malloy's pride and joy was what he called his "knockout" gun. They were taking one big game rifle, to be used only for self-protection if they were attacked by any wild animal. They were not hunters after trophies. How then, Jerry had wondered, were they ever going to bag a yeti which, according to all reports, was swift and elusive and very strong? With the enthusiasm of a small boy showing off a new toy, Malloy demonstrated his special weapon.

It was actually a rifle, but instead of bullets it fired a small syringe tipped with a needle-sharp dart. The syringe contained a drug which, when injected into an animal's blood stream, paralyzed the nervous system temporarily.

"It's a distant cousin to the old Indian blowgun," Malloy said. "They're used on ranches and in zoos and game refuges, on big animals that are too dangerous to handle otherwise. Say a tiger gets sick. This works on him like an anesthetic."

"How fast does it work?"

"Sixty seconds if you hit a vein. About four minutes anywhere else in the body. Knocks them out from twenty minutes up to half an hour, depending on the dose. You figure out your dose in milligrams, according to the size of your animal. It's safe and painless and absolutely humane."

"How far will it shoot?" Jerry asked.

"It's better at short range, around twenty-five yards. Gas operated. We use a carbon dioxide cylinder. If it works on a tiger, it will work on a yeti."

"If you can get that close."

Malloy's jaw set. "I'll get close enough."

Finally the night came when Jerry could write in the official journal: "Today the last packs were made up and weighed. Tomorrow we move them across the valley by truck."

Phari was a small hill village an hour's drive north of Katmandu, located at the end of a rough cart track that passed for a road. Here was the start of the trail, their jumping-off point. From daybreak until dusk Jerry and Malloy shuttled back and forth between the city and the village, hauling loads in a truck borrowed from Rick Dawa's father. By nightfall all the bearers and expedition members had assembled. Tired but jubilant, Jerry climbed down from the cab. Tomorrow was the big day.

Then Malloy called to him. "Six more packs still at the warehouse we couldn't squeeze aboard. Will you drive back for 'em, Dunham?"

He nodded wearily.

"I'd leave it till morning," Malloy said, "but we want to make an early start tomorrow."

"It's all right, Dr. Malloy. I don't mind."

"Grab a bite to eat first. And take Kamin with you. He knows the road."

It was pitch dark by the time Jerry finished eating and a soft, warm rain had set in. He put on his slicker, collected Kamin, and they stepped into the empty truck. The *sirdar* grinned and gave him a thumbs-up gesture as the engine coughed into life. Both knew it was going to be a slow drive at night in the rain. Careful, Dunham, he told himself. That road is no freeway. Easy does it. You can make up your sack time later.

He flicked on the wipers and swung the big truck around in the village street. The yellow lights bored into the drizzle as he eased forward in second gear and the tires churned up gobs of mud. The road snaked around a sharp curve under dripping trees and nosed down toward the valley. They crept along the hillside until the pitch steepened abruptly and Jerry gave the brakes a feather touch with his boot. The pedal went clear to the floorboard.

Gathering speed, the truck bounded from rut to rut. He gave the pedal a desperate jab, but he might have been tramping on air. There were no brakes. He yanked at the emergency, but that too had gone, and now another onrushing curve loomed up in the lights. On his left the hill dropped off into space; on his right a sheer bank hemmed in the road. He fought the wheel and the slick, treacherous mud, trying to hold the truck inside. Beyond that bend, he recalled, the road leveled off. If he could reach that stretch and lose momentum, down shift into low—

"Hold on!" he yelled at Kamin. They rocked around the curve, perilously near the edge on two wheels, and the speedometer needle soared to thirty. The truck teetered, then found traction, and roared into the straightaway. His heart in his throat, he shot into neutral and gunned the motor. The needle fell back to twenty-five, to twenty, and then it happened.

A boulder, loosened by the rain, rolled into the road. He swerved to miss it and the rear wheels went into a wild skid. For one sickening instant they slid toward the drop-off, out of control, and spun back in the other direction. Kamin was thrown violently against him and with a crunch of metal the truck plowed into the bank, hit a rock, and toppled over on its side.

The next few moments were a hazy nightmare. He remembered to switch off the ignition. He felt stiff and sore all over and blood from a cut in his forehead dripped down his face. Beside him Kamin, his eyes shut, moaned softly. He managed to wrench the cab door open and crawl out, but he was too weak to move the Sherpa. Lights from Phari village gleamed above him dimly. He cupped his hands and shouted for help, tottered a few steps up the road, then collapsed in the mud, unconscious.

When he opened his eyes he was lying on a cot in a shack

in the village. Three faces came into focus in the lantern light. Dr. Sebold, Malloy, and Dr. Baimbridge were bending over him. "Feeling better now?" Dr. Sebold asked.

"I—I guess so," he mumbled. "What happened?"

"We heard the crash and carried you back up the hill. You got a nasty bump on the head but nothing serious." Dr. Baimbridge handed him a glass of water and a pill. "Take this."

Jerry swallowed the medicine and shuddered. "The brakes! They wouldn't hold!"

"Never mind that," Dr. Baimbridge said. "You can talk later."

"But what about Kamin? He was hurt, I know he was."

Jerry struggled to sit up but the doctor pushed him firmly down on the cot. "Kamin's all right. The rest of you clear out now. I want to examine this young man a little more thoroughly."

Dr. Sebold and Tom Malloy filed out. Jerry lay back while the doctor poked his ribs and took his pulse. Overhead rain dripped on the thatch roof and wind whispered through the jungle outside. Then he heard Malloy's indignant voice beyond the door. "—crazy reckless kid!" Malloy was saying. "Driving down that grade like a maniac. Can't trust him with a simple errand."

"Keep your voice down, Tom," Dr. Sebold said. "He might hear you."

"Don't care if he does," Malloy snapped. "I tell you, Carl, that Dunham is a menace to the expedition. He's a jinx."

"If you ask me," Dr. Sebold said, "he handled that truck pretty well. Lucky he didn't pile up in the canyon."

"Lucky for him maybe. But not for Kamin."

Dr. Sebold's answer was lost in the wind as the two men moved away, but Malloy's voice carried back in snatches. "—blamed it on the brakes—perfect condition—drove it myself—always has some alibi—excuses—jinx—"

Jerry shut his eyes against the dizziness that swept over him. In his mind he saw the boulder roll down into the road again, heard the crash and Kamin's moans of pain. Had the accident been his fault? Could he have avoided it somehow? "Dr. Baimbridge," he said. "Tell me the truth about Kamin? I have to know."

The doctor looked down at him with sympathy.

"Tell me, Doctor, please."

"Well—" Dr. Baimbridge hesitated. "I'm afraid Kamin snapped his leg when the truck tipped over."

Jerry clenched his fist. Poor Kamin, who had been so anxious to go home, laid up with a broken leg. First there had been the yeti skin. Then Fred Snodgrass in the hospital. And now this. Maybe he, Jerry Dunham, *was* a jinx.

CHAPTER 4

I T was almost noon before Jerry, still drowsy from the effects of the pill, woke up. He had a slight headache but felt fit otherwise. Dressing quickly, he stepped out into the village. From one of the Nepalis he learned that the other *sahibs* had returned to Katmandu, taking Kamin with them. The damaged truck had been towed away. Meanwhile one could only wait. The Nepali shrugged as if to say, *Be patient, it is the will of God.*

Time mattered little to these people, Jerry knew, but it was important to the expedition. Every day counted. By now they should be well on their way, hours into the hills. They would be—except for him.

Long after midday Dr. Sebold and the others drove back into Phari in two jeeps. Malloy looked at Jerry and walked away but Dr. Sebold smiled. "Can't keep a good man down," he said. "How's the head, Jerry?"

"I'm okay. But how's Kamin?"

Kamin's leg, Dr. Sebold told him, had been set in a cast. The Sherpa would stay behind in Katmandu until the bone knit. He was bitterly disappointed, but within a few weeks he would be able to walk as well as ever. Unfortunately too late to join the expedition.

"I feel terrible about this," Jerry said. "If it hadn't been for me—"

"If it hadn't been for you Kamin might be dead. He says your quick thinking was all that saved the truck from skidding over the edge." Dr. Sebold put a hand on his shoulder. "Don't blame yourself. Just be thankful it wasn't worse."

"But Kamin was our head bearer. Can we manage without him?"

"We'll miss him, of course, but I've given Dorje his job, and we'll find another Sherpa somewhere to fill in. Do you feel up to leaving tomorrow?"

Jerry nodded. "If you're sure you want a Jonah like me along."

"Superstitious, are you?" Dr. Sebold laughed. "Don't take Tom Malloy too seriously. He's a good fellow but hot tempered. Doesn't mean half of what he says."

Jerry wasn't so certain of that, but he felt a vast relief. The expedition had been delayed one day, but Dr. Sebold did not hold him responsible. Only Tom Malloy did. Well, he would have to get along with Malloy somehow, put up with his temper. And hereafter be doubly careful.

Rick caught his eye then, and said, "Let's take a walk. I want to talk to you—alone."

The two boys crossed the village and climbed up among the trees for some distance, until Rick stopped on a ridge that overlooked the road. "Now, friend Jerry," he said, "tell me about that accident. From the beginning. Everything you can remember."

Jerry recounted the details, from the moment he had arrived in Phari last night until the crash. After he finished Rick was silent, rubbing his chin thoughtfully. Then he said, "When Malloy asked you to drive back into town did anybody else hear him?"

"They could have," Jerry said. "There must have been fifty men waiting to help unload the packs."

"But when you came out after eating was anybody near the truck?"

"Not a soul. They'd all ducked inside out of the rain." Mystified, Jerry stared at his friend. He'd never seen him look so serious. "Why? Is something wrong?"

"I'm not sure yet," Rick said grimly. "But while you were gone anyone could have tampered with the truck and not been seen."

"Tampered?"

"That truck was serviced three days ago by my father's mechanics. When we hauled it into the garage this morning there wasn't a drop of fluid in the brake system."

"It probably leaked out."

"There's no leak. Those brakes worked fine yesterday and then all of a sudden they let go. It wouldn't take five minutes with a pair of pliers to drain the line."

It was possible, Jerry admitted reluctantly to himself. He had parked the truck under a tree and left it unguarded for a good thirty minutes in the dark. Possible, yes, but fantastic. "Why would anybody set out to wreck your father's truck?" he said. "It doesn't make sense."

"The truck was only part of it," Rick said. "Maybe they wanted to get the driver."

"Me?" Jerry grinned. "Public Enemy Number One?"

"Go ahead, laugh. I know it sounds crazy. But I'm going to keep snooping."

"I'm not laughing, Rick. I just can't believe anybody would deliberately try to harm me. Why should they?"

"There's a reason. There has to be."

"Have you mentioned this to Dr. Sebold?"

"No. He wouldn't believe me either. He trusts everybody. But this is Nepal, not the U.S.A." Rick added, "I can't prove a thing. Yet."

"Come on," Jerry said. "You have a hunch, though. Tell me." But Rick refused to discuss the subject further. He said he had one last errand in Katmandu. They walked back to the village and he roared off in a jeep.

After he had gone Jerry found it was not so easy to dismiss Rick's suspicions as the product of a wild imagination. Malloy himself had said the brakes were in perfect condition. As much as Malloy seemed to dislike him, the scientist wouldn't lie about such a matter. The longer he struggled for an answer, the more confused he became. The guilty person, if there was one, must be some villager not connected with the expedition. But the why of it remained a mystery, unless Rick could sniff out the truth.

He didn't see Rick again until next morning. Rick merely winked and shook his head, and in the scramble to get off Jerry had no chance to question him. They ate a hurried breakfast before daybreak and rolled up their sleeping gear. The porters shouldered their packs, laughing and joking. Dorje, the new *sirdar*, organized them into a column that stretched for a quarter mile. Everyone was excited, eager to start. The months of planning and preparation were all behind. Ahead lay—what?

Dr. Sebold walked to the head of the long line. As the sun rose over the eastern hills he waved his hat, then turned into the trail. Jerry peered up at the green slopes, gave his shoulder straps a final hitch, and strode after him. The expedition was under way at last.

It was a beautiful morning, clear and crisp, and Dr. Sebold set an easy pace. They climbed through forests of feathery bamboo and rhododendron and other plants unknown to Jerry, passed by tiny fields planted in corn and buckwheat, and entered an occasional village clinging to the steep hillsides. But he was more interested in the fauna. In the mud on either side he kept looking for animal tracks. Gradually the heat increased and they stopped to rest beside a small icy mountain creek.

"Good morning, young *sahib*," a voice said behind him.

Jerry turned. A short dark man gave him a gilt-toothed grin. It was Ang Nuri, the Sherpa from Sikkim.

"Surprise to see me, yes I think," Ang Nuri chuckled. "But here I am."

Sweat glistened on his face and a pack rode high on his back. "Are you our new bearer?" Jerry asked.

Ang bobbed his head. "Now have job with Americans. Find many yeti."

Jerry tried to recall their conversation in the Katmandu bazaar the week before. What was it Ang had said? "Maybe somebody get sick." It was just coincidence, the sort you always heard about in India, but the Sherpa's manner puzzled him. "Did you know Kamin broke his leg?"

"Oh yes. Too bad. Very sad for Kamin."

One of the Nepalis kneeling beside the creek to drink let out an excited cry and pointed. *"Kang-mi!"* he shouted.

Jerry rushed up the bank with several others. There in the soft dirt was the imprint of a huge paw. It was narrow, something like the shape of a human foot, but with clawmarks. Dr. Sebold crouched down. "It's not our snowman," he said. "Might be a Himalayan bear. What do you think, Tom?"

Jerry held his breath while Malloy examined the track.

"You're right, Carl," Malloy said. *"Ursus selenarctos thibetanus,* the Asiatic black bear. Seldom goes above the treeline. Notice the prominent hallux and the dwarf fifth digit."

"Looks like an African mountain gorilla," Dr. Sebold said.

"These Himalayan bruins make a pug that resembles a primate. That's why identification fools the experts sometimes.

Isabellinus, that's the one to look out for. Red bear. He's savage, a mauler, like our grizzly."

"Isn't his habitat Tibet?"

"He ranges this side too. Up to twenty thousand feet. Very rare. Some people believe he's the yeti."

"We'll keep our eyes peeled," Dr. Sebold said. "Better luck next time."

Ang Nuri plucked at Jerry's sleeve. "You see, young *sahib,*" he whispered. "Is good sign. Ang Nuri bring much luck."

The column got under way again and climbed on without incident. They saw no more tracks or game of any kind, although Rick sighted a blood pheasant, a bird with brilliant red and green plumage. Late that afternoon they reached another village, where the head man welcomed them warmly, and pitched camp on the outskirts. They had made good distance for the first day and Jerry found he was glad to seek his cot after supper.

He was writing up the expedition journal when Rick slipped into the tent. "Be sure and shake out your boots before you put them on again," Rick said.

"All right, but why?"

"We have all sorts of wildlife in Nepal." Rick tapped an empty boot. A pale worm-like creature fell out and wriggled away. "Leeches. Five or six of those can hold a pint of blood. Your blood."

"Ugh." Jerry inspected his other boot but it was free of the parasites. Lowering his voice, he said, "Did you learn any more about the truck?"

"No, but I haven't given up. I see Dr. Sebold hired that Sikkim porter to fill in."

"I guess he didn't have much choice. All the other Sherpas were signed up for the Swiss and British expeditions." Jerry looked at him curiously. "You don't suspect Ang Nuri? He wasn't there when it happened."

"I suspect everybody," Rick said darkly. "There'd better not be any more 'accidents.' "

As the expedition pushed ahead the country grew wilder and more mountainous. Villages were fewer and the rivers were great milky torrents fed by melting snows. But of snow itself, or the Himalayas, Jerry had no glimpse. Range after range of pine-clad hills, separated by deep gorges, cut off the view. It reminded him of his own Rockies and rapidly he got his "mountain legs" back, so that he could climb for hours without tiring.

The fourth evening out they were met by a native runner with the message that a site for the expedition base camp had been found several days march to the northeast. The big news, however, was that two yetis had been reported in the district. That night they sat up late around the campfire discussing what to do when and if they actually came upon fresh tracks.

The Sherpas, Jerry discovered, were fearless when it came to climbing mountains, but most were deathly afraid of yetis. A few claimed that yetis ate human flesh and carried off children to their lairs. But Dr. Sebold insisted they were harmless and equally afraid of humans. They did eat the meat of small animals which they caught; they also ate berries and roots and lived in caves. His theory was that they were similar to the great apes, although more intelligent, because none ever had been caught.

Malloy pointed out that some Sherpas believed the yetis were a sect of Tibetan monks called *lung-gompa*, or holy runners, who wore no clothes and never cut their hair, and ran when anyone came near. They were said to live on bugs and salt which collected on lichen-covered rocks at snowline. This way they acquired heavenly merit for the life hereafter.

Ross Howe, the anthropologist, had still another theory. He believed the yeti was a low form of primitive man, the last survivor of some race that went back half a million years. They were known to play games with rocks, they had semi-human voices, they cleaned their meat before eating it. No animals did these things. They lived in the Himalayas because this was the most inaccessible and, for them, the safest place on earth.

"What about you, Jerry?" someone asked. "Everybody has his own pet theory on the abominable snowman."

Jerry shook his head. Bear? Ape? Holy monk? Prehistoric man? "After all this talk," he said, "I'm ready to believe almost anything."

He was to prove that statement sooner than he knew.

Next morning he got up early, as usual, and loaded a roll of film into his camera. Planning to take some snapshots of camp, he climbed a low ridge, found a pleasing angle, and got a light-meter reading. When he looked up his heart gave a leap. A thing—something with long brown hair and bright eyes was peering at him from a thicket not ten yards away.

At first he thought it must be a langur monkey, which many

scientists believed to be the real yeti. But when the creature moved he saw it had no tail. In fact it looked human, standing upright, about four and a half feet tall. Hardly daring to breathe, he eased his camera into position. The creature, partially screened by brush, looked poised for flight. Should he call down to camp? Would his shout frighten it away? Was there any way to lure it closer, or even capture it?

He snapped the picture. With the click of the shutter the animal, or whatever it was, whirled and bounded off. Jerry gave a yell to alert the others and ran after it. He caught one more glimpse of a shaggy figure and then it vanished into the trees. It ran erect like a man, not on all fours, with amazing speed, never glancing back.

He raced on, tripping over vines and logs, until he was out of wind and could run no more. His quarry had disappeared completely, although he could imagine it peering at him through the forest gloom from some hideaway. Nor could he find a single track on the thick mat of pine needles. It was eerie, almost as if he had imagined the whole affair. He retraced his route, hunting for tufts of fur or hair or any sign at all, but there were none.

Shortly several of the men came panting up the ridge. "What was it?" Dr. Sebold asked.

"I don't know," Jerry admitted and described his experience. "I guess it could have been a yeti."

Tom Malloy snorted. "Not at this elevation. They've never been reported below twelve thousand feet."

Nevertheless Dr. Sebold ordered a search, and a score of natives spread out across the forest and advanced in a line.

After an hour or so, when no trace had been found, Jerry felt more sheepish than ever.

"Let me have that film," Howe suggested. "I'll develop it tonight and see if you got anything."

Jerry turned over the camera to him without much hope, but at that night's camp Howe set up his darkroom tent and got out his developing trays and mixed his solutions. After what seemed like hours, but was only minutes, he removed the damp strip of film and hung it up to dry. For some while the anthropologist studied the negative through a glass, turning it this way and that, until Jerry was ready to explode with impatience.

"Did you ever hear of the *Hajus?*" Howe said finally.

"No, sir."

"Not many people have," Howe went on. "And fewer have ever seen one. As you found out this morning, they're mighty shy."

"But what are they?"

"*Haju,*" Howe said, "means 'forest wizard' in the local dialect. They're one of the aboriginal tribes who inhabit these mountains. Wild, very simple, still pretty much Stone Age in their culture. But they're as human as you and I."

"But he was naked, covered with long hair," Jerry said.

"That's the way they live. They migrate with the seasons like some animals. In winter you'll find them down in the warm jungle."

Jerry peered at the negative. He could see now, as the camera's eye had recorded it, that his creature did resemble a man, although not a very handsome specimen. Disgusted at himself, he said, "Then it's not even first cousin to a yeti?"

"Afraid not, Jerry." Howe's smile was friendly. "Anybody might make the same mistake. Let's call it the big one that got away."

CHAPTER 5

THE weather had turned cooler as they gained altitude and next morning a thin coat of ice crusted the water buckets. At ten thousand feet Jerry slipped into his sheepskin jacket for the first time. Two hours after breaking camp they plodded to the summit of a pass and a breath-taking panorama of the Himalayas suddenly spread before his eyes.

From west to east the great chain of white peaks loomed in the sun, dominated by the pyramid of Everest and its plume of wind-blown snow. Rick identified the others for him—Annapurna, Makalu, Shaulagiri, and distant Kanchenjunga—giants all, that stretched across the northern horizon in a massive, jagged wall. He stared in awe, wondering how puny man had managed to scale any single one. And he began to understand how these mountains could hide their secret of the yeti. Here was a wilderness of ice and rock so vast it stunned the mind.

For the Sherpas this was a joyous moment. They placed stones on the cairn at the summit and broke into song. Every member of the expedition, Jerry thought, must feel his pulse quicken at the sight. They had come a long way and those peaks marked their goal.

The remainder of the journey passed quickly. On the tenth day they crossed the Balu Kosi River on a swaying suspension bridge, barely wide enough for one man, and climbed into a narrow mountain-ringed valley. It was an alpine meadow, carpeted with grass and wild flowers. A glacier thrust its icy snout into the upper end. A village clung to the ridge overlooking the valley and above that perched the fortress-like walls of a lamasery.

With a shout of welcome a tall fair-haired man stepped from a tent and strode forward. It was John Conrad, biologist and expedition advance man, who had set up their base camp here at fourteen thousand feet. Greeting everyone at once, he shook hands with Jerry and introduced himself, then led the way back into camp. "How do you like the view?" he said.

Carl Sebold peered up at the peaks. "Magnificent, John," he said. "You picked a good one."

"I thought you'd like it," Conrad said. "And not only the scenery. There's plenty of water, firewood, protection from the wind, a village nearby. All we need now is a yeti or two."

"What about the report you sent us?"

"It's firsthand," Conrad said. "I talked to the man himself, a yak herder. He insists he saw two yetis above snowline. He was so terrified he came down that glacier after dark."

"Sounds promising," Dr. Sebold said. "We'll try up there first thing."

The last of the Nepalis straggled in before sundown with their packs. Every man was accounted for. Tons of equipment had been transported over the long rough trail from Phari without loss or damage. The expedition, save for Fred Snodgrass, was intact, ready to strike off into the unknown.

Much to Jerry's disappointment, however, they did not push on for several days. As Dr. Sebold explained, they had to allow their bodies time to adjust to the altitude. Mountain sickness could be a real hazard to climbers. Also there was work to be done. The gear had to be unpacked and re-sorted and stored in weatherproof tents. The tents had to be guyed and reinforced with rocks against the violent storms that sometimes swept down from Tibet. Most of the Nepalis had to be paid off for their return journey, since only a few would be needed in camp.

Next they must pay a courtesy visit to the abbot of the lamasery. According to Rick he was the most important man in the district, worshipped by the Sherpas, and nothing could be undertaken without his approval. So Jerry and the others climbed up through the village to the lamasery, Terang Gompa. A red-robed lama led them into a courtyard and through a room lined with big leather cylinders mounted on spindles.

As they passed their guide gave each cylinder a turn. "Prayer drums," Rick explained to Jerry. "Each drum contains thousands of pieces of paper with a prayer written on it."

"Is that why the lama turned them?" Jerry asked.

"That's right. The Sherpas are very devout. They believe that every time you revolve one of those drums you're saying your prayers several thousand times. And you have to turn from right to left or the prayers don't count."

The abbot, an old man with great dignity, received them in a room hung with religious scrolls. Tea was served and after Dr. Sebold made a speech, which Rick translated into the native tongue, they presented their gifts. In turn the abbot presented each with a strip of white cloth. "These are *kata* scarves," Rick said. "They're sacred now because the abbot has blessed them. It means he's blessed the expedition, too, and wishes us well."

"Thank him, Rick," Dr. Sebold said. "And tell him we're grateful."

Rick spoke a few words and then listened while the abbot talked at length. "He also wishes to warn us," Rick interpreted.

"Warn us? About what?"

"We are only a few miles from the Tibetan border. Several Red military patrols have been seen on this side the past few months. They have no business here but he urges us to be careful whenever we climb in that direction."

"Ask him about yetis," Malloy said.

At the word "yeti" a smile came to the old man's face. He spoke to one of the monks, who left the room and returned a minute later with a piece of reddish brown fur shaped like a cone. A band of darker fur about an inch wide ran up the front and back, meeting at the crown. "A yeti scalp," Rick said. "It was at Terang Gompa when the abbot first came here many years ago. He has no idea how old it is."

Malloy gave a startled exclamation. Everyone crowded around to examine the object. It was certainly genuine. The hairs looked and felt exactly like those on the skin that had been lost in New York.

"Amazing!" Dr. Sebold said. "It's one more bit of evidence. No animal on earth has a skull like this."

"Ask if he'll sell it," Malloy said to Rick.

"I'm sure he won't."

"Go ahead and ask," Malloy insisted. "Tell him we'll pay well."

Rick proved to be right. The abbot granted permission to take photographs, but said it was a relic of the lamasery and not for sale. Malloy had to be content with a promise that he could return next day and take as many pictures as he wished.

They said goodbye and climbed back down the trail. When they reached camp Rick drew Jerry aside. "Why was Malloy so anxious to buy that scalp?" he said. "I know he was able to get a piece of yeti hide two years ago."

"It's gone now," Jerry said, and told about the incident in the New York hotel.

"You never mentioned that before."

"It's past history," Jerry said. "Something I'd just as soon forget."

"The abbot knew about it. He told me: 'A relic of great value has been lost. Until it is found your friends will suffer misfortune.'"

"How could he know?" Jerry demanded. "That happened weeks ago, ten thousand miles from here."

"I can't explain it, Jerry, but some of these holy men have strange powers. And you'll have to admit, we've had more than our share of bad luck so far."

"A jinx?" Jerry shook his head. "With all respect to your lama, I don't believe in such things."

"I don't either." Rick frowned. "Just the same I wish that skin would turn up. I have a funny feeling it's important somehow."

And so the matter was left—one more unsolved riddle in the mystery of the abominable snowman.

By the fifth day after their arrival Dr. Sebold felt they were ready to take the field. He divided the expedition into two teams: himself, Jerry, Rick, and Ross Howe in Team One. Tom Malloy, Dr. Baimbridge, Lars Johansen, and John Conrad in Team Two. Each was assigned four Sherpa and five Nepali bearers. In addition Rick persuaded Nemi, the yak herder who had sighted the yetis, to accompany Team One and point out the exact spot.

Early next morning they shouldered their packs and headed up the valley. This first trip was to be a reconnaissance, scouting the lay of the land, and at the foot of the glacier the two teams separated. Dr. Sebold's group turned west and climbed up through meadows where yaks grazed under the watchful eye of their herdsmen. Slowly the camp tents dwindled to tiny white dots far below and grass gave way to rock.

And now Jerry began to realize the importance of conditioning. The Sherpas climbed tirelessly, while everyone else was puffing and blowing, fighting for oxygen. Rick assured him, however, that in another week or two his lungs would work like bellows. He was surprised, also, at the abundance of animal life in this seemingly barren country. They came upon marmots, rabbits, voles and, with the aid of binoculars, spotted herds of bharal and ibex on the distant skyline.

Having detoured around the glacier, they camped that night far above timber line and built a windbreak of stones beside a small lake. Dog tired, Jerry crawled into his down bag and fell asleep at once.

After breakfast Nemi grew uneasy and muttered to himself. "*Kharab rasta,*" he said and shook his head.

"What's he saying, Rick?" Dr. Sebold asked.

"He says it's a bad route ahead," Rick explained. "He doesn't want to go any farther."

Nemi's story was that one of his yaks had strayed; otherwise he never would have gone this way. In trying to follow it he had climbed around a boulder and come face to face with two yetis. They had jumped up and down in rage, growled at him, and picked up rocks as if to throw. Nemi had turned and run in terror. His yak never had been found.

As he told of the experience he began to tremble, and refused to answer any more questions. But he finally agreed to lead the party nearer to the scene, in return for more *bakshish*. The loss of a yak, he said, had made him a poor man and he needed money.

Leaving all the porters behind in camp, they rounded the lake and clambered up toward the nearest snowfield. Presently

Nemi halted and pointed toward a ridge above. Nothing would induce him to go another step. The rest climbed on over the crusted snow and down into a hollow. "There they are!" Rick shouted.

Jerry stared down at the double line of prints which led off into a jumble of boulders, and his breath caught. They were like no footmarks he had ever seen, blurred and very large, about twenty inches long and ten inches wide. "They must have been huge," he said. "Bigger than a silvertip grizzly!"

"You'd think so," Dr. Sebold said. "That's how some of these wild yarns about the yeti's size have started. But this pair probably was no larger than four or five feet tall."

"How can you tell?"

"We know these tracks are several weeks old. In that length of time the action of sun and wind on the snow changes them. They must be two or three times larger than the original tracks."

Rick chuckled. "The originals were big enough to scare poor Nemi. And they were probably as scared as he was."

"I'm afraid they'll be a long way from here by now," Dr. Sebold said. "But maybe we can learn something."

The tracks were plain and easy to follow, for no recent snow had fallen to cover them. At one place Dr. Sebold pointed out where the yetis had broken into a run, because their tracks were farther apart and deeper. Behind a rock he paused again to examine the shattered bones of a snow partridge. It was possible, he said, that yetis had killed and eaten the partridge.

"That's another puzzler about these creatures. They appear

to be omnivorous. But none of the ape family is. The bear is one of the few mammals that eats both meat and vegetable matter."

"How would they catch a bird?" Jerry asked.

"They'd have to be wonderfully quick hunters. But that's only a guess. And guesswork, Jerry, isn't a very reliable basis on which to make a scientific deduction. The truth is, we have too many theories and legends, and too few facts."

"At least we know yetis are highly intelligent."

"Whatever they are, they've outwitted the best human hunters so far."

The tracks turned up a steep, slippery slope, so the group paused to buckle crampons on their boots. Fifteen minutes later they topped out on a windswept crest where all trace of snow had been scoured away. Here the trail ended at bare rock. They split into pairs, Jerry and Dr. Sebold climbing a draw to the left, with Rick and Howe ascending to the right. The first to pick up the trail again was to signal the other by walkie-talkie.

"You know what the word 'yeti' means, don't you?" Dr. Sebold asked.

"Snowman?" Jerry said.

"No, it means 'Thing of the rocky places.' The rocks are his natural habitat. Not snow. Some newspaperman dreamed up that 'snowman' name for a publicity stunt, and it stuck."

As they walked along, searching for more tracks, Dr. Sebold told him the Sherpas believed there were three kinds of yeti. The first was called a *yalmo*, a fearsome giant fifteen feet tall. The second stood about eight feet. The third and most common, the *longhi*, was described as smaller than the average man, about the size of a fourteen-year-old boy. The first two, he suspected, were myths. But the *longhi* was evidently real.

"After all," he said, "something made those tracks. If we're smart enough to find out what—"

The draw led them up to another snowfield, but its surface was smooth and unbroken. No prints were in sight. From time to time Jerry got in touch with the other two by radio, but they had found no sign either. The yetis seemed to have vanished into space. Although it was not yet noon he noticed how cold the day had grown, and the sky was turning an ugly gray.

He was pulling on his gloves when static crackled in his ears and Howe's excited voice spoke from the walkie-talkie. "Can you read me, Jerry?"

Jerry pressed the button. "Loud and clear. Where are you now?"

"Up the ridge. Come quick! We've found more tracks. Fresh ones. They can't be two days old!"

"Wait for us. We're on our way."

Jerry telescoped his aerial and followed Dr. Sebold at a trot. A long climb brought them to the ridge top where they sighted Rick and Howe. Plowing on through deep snow, they overtook the others within a few minutes. Howe was busy photographing the prints while Rick had out tape and notebook to record their measurements.

These were the tracks of a single yeti, much smaller than the double set they had followed earlier, and they led toward a saddle between two peaks. The edges were clear and sharply defined, which indicated they had been made recently. "I'd guess we're not twenty-four hours behind this one," Howe said.

Dr. Sebold nodded. "He's heading for that pass. I'll make another guess and say that we've run across one of the routes they use regularly."

"The question is," said Howe, "how many miles are we behind. Do we stand a chance of catching him?"

Jerry peered up at a band of rocks. It was possible they were closer than they dared to imagine, that the yeti had doubled back to spy on them and even now was lying concealed somewhere nearby.

"A chance, maybe. But a long one, I think. Remember, he can run circles around us." Dr. Sebold craned his neck. "Take a look at that sky."

Dark clouds had formed over the peaks and a gust of icy wind swept along the ridge. Something cold stung Jerry's cheek and he raised a hand to his face. It was a pellet of snow. "Maybe it's only a flurry," he said without much hope.

"Looks more like a storm blowing up," Howe said. "How about it, Rick? You're our weather prophet."

Rick moistened a finger tip and held it to the wind. "From the north. That usually means a storm. Up here you can expect one any time."

They all looked at Dr. Sebold. He was the leader. He had to make the decision. Jerry didn't envy him. This was a tough one: to go on, or turn back, and risk losing the yeti's trail. "I hate to quit now," he said.

Nobody else spoke. Flakes drifted down faster, drawing a white curtain across the skyline. Already Jerry felt the chill creeping into his boots. He stamped his feet and beat his hands together, while Dr. Sebold peered up at the threatening sky. Jerry could almost read his mind. *What rotten luck. No snow for weeks but the minute we find fresh tracks it starts in.*

Finally he said, "We can't gamble on the weather. It might clear off in an hour or set in for days." Dr. Sebold sighed. "I'm afraid we're licked this time."

Without a word they turned their backs to the storm. Jerry had one last glimpse of the footprints before he started down for camp. As he trudged on through the drifts, this seemed the bitterest disappointment yet.

CHAPTER 6

FORTUNATELY the wind did not increase and, by following their own tracks, they reached the lakeside camp well before dark. Worried by their long absence, Dorje came out to meet them with a thermos of hot tea. Snow continued to fall that night and the following day, so they had no choice but to burrow into their tents and keep as warm as possible. Snug in their bags, Jerry and Rick passed the time writing letters, talking about yetis, and speculating whether Team Two had enjoyed better luck.

As Rick pointed out, there was one consolation. On their first try they had found a fresh sign. They should consider that an omen of future success.

64

The storm died during the second night and next day they crawled out into a world of dazzling white. A foot of new snow covered the rocks and all but the center of the lake had frozen over. Jerry spent the morning catching up on his journal, while Dr. Sebold and Howe climbed up toward what they jokingly called "Yeti Pass." They returned that afternoon, blue-lipped with cold, to report that the snow was so deep and soft they had been unable to break through.

"Can we try again tomorrow?" Jerry asked.

"You know the old saying, 'Haste makes waste.' I think we'd be wasting our time. Those tracks are covered deep."

"But what if that yeti comes back?"

"We'll be back too, Jerry. But we only have three days' food left. And I want to be sure that Team Two came through the storm all right. Tomorrow we're going down to base camp."

He was right, Jerry realized. As director Dr. Sebold had to play it safe and think of the expedition's welfare first, no matter how badly he wanted to push on. "I told you once we're like a military unit. A vest-pocket army. Every army has to retreat sometimes. That's what this is, a tactical retreat."

They made the descent to Terang in one day. After the frigid air of the high country their valley seemed tropical by comparison. Malloy's team had not returned yet, nor sent back a runner with news, and Jerry could not establish contact by radio. This was no cause for alarm, but he sensed Dr. Sebold's concern.

He set up the short-wave receiver and tuned in the government station at New Delhi, far across the hills and down on the sweltering plains of India. Reception was poor because of static, but a voice crackled across the miles, first in Hindustani and Urdu and then in English. Both short- and long-range weather forecasts were favorable. Meteorologists predicted fair skies and normal temperatures, with no more storms in the offing.

With a smile of relief Jerry handed the report to Dr. Sebold. Good weather was the break they needed most. But the news broadcast, which followed, was not so good.

A demonstration led by Communists, according to the announcer, had broken out in the streets of Katmandu. They had torn down an American flag. Extra police had been mobilized to prevent rioting. The situation in the capital remained tense.

Rick shook his head. "You see now why it was so important for the expedition to hurry," he said gravely. "If we had been there when this happened—"

"But why," Jerry said, "are the Reds demonstrating against us?"

Rick unrolled a map of Asia. "Simple geography. Nepal is the gateway between India and Red Tibet. Someday they hope to control that gate. But they can't so long as we Nepalese are friendly to your country."

"Go on."

"The Communists do everything they can to hurt American influence. They talk against you, try to make all Americans look bad to my people. They are very clever and determined. And dangerous."

"So this is how they stir up trouble?"

"This is one of their many ways," Rick said. "You see,

Nepal is small, and they are huge. We cannot hold them off alone. We need American support. And you need us."

"At least we're out of trouble here in Terang."

"Don't be too sure of that."

The news broadcast made no mention of the rioting the next two nights, and Rick soon forgot it in his anxiety about Team Two. For Malloy's party was now overdue. The fourth morning after their return he and Dr. Sebold and two Sherpas climbed up the valley on Team Two's trail. About noon they sighted a row of specks up the cliffs and presently the two groups met.

The men looked exhausted and Tom Malloy's face was glum. "Not a sign of tracks," he reported disgustedly. "Over a week up there and nothing to show for it."

"You got back safely," Dr. Sebold said. "That's more important."

Malloy's account was discouraging. They had camped near the seventeen-thousand-foot level and scoured the area. Even after the storm they had stayed on, struggling against snow and extreme cold as they climbed higher. They had been forced to turn back when their food ran out. By that time, also, Baimbridge and Johansen had begun to suffer from altitude.

Back at base camp the four tired members of Team Two rolled into their bags, and the Sherpas talked in low voices around the cook fire. There was no feast to celebrate their reunion that night. Jerry could feel the air of gloom, almost as if they had a foreboding of trouble to come.

Next morning Dr. Sebold called the group together and

outlined his new plan. The expedition would move in force up to the lake camp for a more intensive search of that region. They would fan out in small teams and concentrate on the pass, which he was convinced the yetis used to cross from one side of the range to the other. Only Lars Johansen would remain behind at Terang, to collect botanical specimens.

This meant packing up more supplies and equipment than they'd taken on the first reconnaissance. Each man would have to carry a sixty-pound load. "We'll take off two days from now," he said. "I want you Team Two fellows to rest up."

"We don't need rest," Malloy protested. "We're ready any time."

"Not everybody is as rugged as you are, Tom," Dr. Sebold said mildly.

"But we'll lose two days. We can't afford to sit here in camp."

"We can't afford to have anybody sick, either. I want you all at full strength for the next push. So rest it is."

The delay pleased Rick. It gave him, he told Jerry, his first real opportunity to examine the bird life, which was his hobby. Carrying binoculars and camera, they climbed down the valley for the day. "Malloy was just the same two years ago," Rick said when they were out of earshot of camp. "Always driving himself and his men."

It was the first time he had spoken of that earlier expedition, and Jerry said curiously, "Was he the leader of it?"

"No. He's a brilliant scientist. But when it comes to yetis he's a fanatic."

"How so?"

"He has a kind of obsession about them. Bound to catch one—or else. Nothing's going to stop him."

"Well, isn't that why we're here?"

"Sure. And it's fine to be dedicated to your work. But that man has a one-track mind." Rick grinned suddenly. "Let's talk about something more fun. Today, if we're lucky, I'll show you one of the world's most amazing birds."

They left the trail and soon found a spot to Rick's liking—a bald rocky knob above the creek. Back among the trees he fashioned a small blind out of branches, behind which he and Jerry could lie, and tossed out a rabbit carcass as bait. He set up the camera in a niche among the rocks and from it ran a trip line to the blind.

Jerry had photographed wild animals from concealment before, but never had he seen such patience as Rick displayed. Hour after hour they lay motionless and silent, watching the rocks and the timber beyond. One of the first birds to appear was strikingly marked, with a red bill, white wings, gray mantle, and a black crescent on its chest. On long legs it waded into the stream.

"Tibetan *ibis*," Rick whispered. "Very rare."

They saw gaudy crimson and lavender wall creepers, fluttering along the cliffs like butterflies. They saw red and yellow sunbirds, flycatchers, shrikes, and a dozen other varieties unknown to Jerry, but none approached the carcass. As morning passed and the afternoon wore on, he wondered with mounting puzzlement what his friend could be waiting for.

The sun was about to slide behind the western canyon wall when Rick finally nudged him. Peering up, he saw a tiny speck high in the sky. It hovered and dipped and circled, steadily gliding lower, then plunged down toward the rocks. An enormous bird, with distinctive black and white markings and a wingspread of almost ten feet, swooped overhead with a whistle of feathers, snatched the rabbit carcass in its talons, and flew away.

"You didn't take the picture," Jerry said.

"Wait. Don't move."

The bird soared up in a spiral and let the meat drop. With a heavy thud it fell back onto the rock. Once again the great bird descended and pounced on the meat, rending savagely with its hooked beak and picking out the splintered bones. It was an ugly creature, with a tuft of shiny feathers that waggled like an old man's beard as it ate. After watching for some while, Rick tripped his camera shutter and the bird flapped off in alarm, climbing rapidly until it vanished.

"Was I seeing things?" Jerry said. "Or did that monster really have chin whiskers?"

"It's the bearded lammergeier, sort of a cross between the eagle and the vulture. Not many other birds have a larger wingspan."

"Why did it drop the carcass?"

"To break the bones so they'd be small enough to swallow. Believe it or not, the lammergeier has been sighted as high as twenty-seven thousand feet. The Sherpas have a lot of legends about its strength, but nobody knows much about its habits."

"I'll bet you'd rather catch one than a yeti."

Rick laughed. "No, I like to see the wild things free. Photographing is enough thrill for me."

In the dusk they hurried back to camp. While Rick went off with Howe to develop his film, Jerry ate a hasty supper and tuned in the short wave for the nightly weather report. It was dark by the time he finished and yellow candlelight glowed through the tents. The Sherpas and Nepalis had bedded down early, as was their habit, and the only sound was the rumble of the creek.

The two big supply tents had been pitched at the end of the row and he strolled toward them, intending to get a fresh battery for the radio. A soft, scurrying noise brought him to a halt. It came from the farther tent. *Mouse,* he thought, and grinned to himself. *You'll get slim pickings there, my friend. Everything is sealed up tight.*

As he started forward again his foot rattled against a loose stone. There was a startled hiss of breath and a bulky dark shape hurtled out of the tent flap and ran off. Jerry was so astounded that for a second he stood open-mouthed, staring into the night. He was about to shout and changed his mind. After the ribbing he'd taken over the Haju, he didn't want to risk another. But one thing sure, he thought grimly: this visitor had been a man, the human kind, not a snowman.

He snapped on his flashlight and stepped out into the meadow. The tracks led across dew-drenched grass and vanished at the rocky creek bed. The man couldn't be far ahead, but which way had he turned—upstream or down? He took a chance on up, toward the glacial moraine, a great pile of boulders and gravel deposited by the glacier as it receded over the years. There a man could lose himself easily.

Carefully picking his way, he followed the creek for several hundred yards. It twisted back and forth between steep banks and he had to ford several times. Soon he was soaked to the knees and his teeth were chattering. But presently his stubbornness paid off. He came upon a wet bootprint on a flat rock. His quarry was only minutes, or possibly seconds, ahead.

For the first time it occurred to him that the man might be dangerous. He had been foolish not to summon help. Now it was too late. His shouts could not be heard back at camp above the roaring water. He could not even see camp now, but only a distant pinprick of light from Terang village on the ridge above. He clambered up the bank to a higher vantage point and stopped to listen, shivering in the wind.

Huge boulders loomed on either side, ghostly gray shapes in the starlight. He realized his flashlight beam warned the man of his presence, and he snapped off the switch. Now the night was blacker than ever but he no longer felt so exposed. Two could play at this game.

Wait, his instinct told him. *Be patient. This is not a wild animal you're stalking.* Crouched behind a rock, he wondered who the intruder could be. He thought of Rick's suspicions about the truck accident. Could there be some connection?

Once again he had the crawly sensation that somebody was watching him. He turned his head slightly. *There!* A faint shadow had changed shape beside the next boulder. Or was it an optical illusion of his nerves?

Off to his left rock suddenly thudded against rock. Jerry leaped up and whirled around. He could see nothing, hear nothing but the pounding of his heart. His body seemed to freeze as he strained to peer into the darkness. Then the sound of footsteps scraping on rock came from his right, toward the creek. He swung back in time to see a dark figure, bent double, plunge over the bank and disappear.

He knew he'd been fooled by an old trick. The man had tossed a stone in one direction to divert his attention, then slipped off the opposite way. With a yell he took after him at a run. He scrambled down the bank, stumbled on some gravel, and fell headlong. The flashlight dropped from his hand and struck a rock with a tinkle of shattered glass. His ears still ringing, he got to his feet with a gasp of pain and almost fell again. He had twisted his ankle.

Downstream someone splashed across the creek and running footsteps dwindled into silence. Jerry hobbled a few steps and sat down to take weight off his ankle. In this shape he'd never catch the man. He'd let his quarry outwit him and escape. He should return to camp at once and soak that ankle, maybe tape it up. Angry and disgusted, he limped on down the creek.

As he emerged at the edge of the meadow a light bobbed across the grass, coming toward him. The beam shone in his eyes and Malloy's voice said, "Dunham! What in thunder are you wandering about in the dark for?"

"I broke my flash," Jerry said. "What are you doing?"

"I was out for a walk and saw a light. Thought I'd better investigate."

"Did you see or hear anybody? He must have run past you."

"Nobody's been by here."

"Did you come straight from camp, or up the creek?"

"From camp, of course. Say, what is this?"

Jerry told him about the prowler he had surprised in the supply tent, how he had chased the man, and then lost him when he twisted his ankle. After Malloy had heard the story he said, "That's odd. You wait here while I climb up and look around."

In fifteen minutes he returned to report that he had found nothing, not even a wet bootprint on the rocks. There was no point, he said, in rousing the whole camp to make a search. By now the prowler, whoever he was, would be far away. Deep in thought, Jerry accompanied him back to the supply tents. They lit a lantern and inspected the orderly rows of spare equipment. No boxes had been broken open and nothing seemed to be missing.

Malloy scratched his head and turned to him with a frown. "Everything checks out. Are you sure you didn't imagine this?"

"I'm sure."

"Then it must have been some would-be sneak thief from the village that you scared off. Those people are terribly poor."

Jerry remembered Nemi, the yak herder. There were other villagers equally poor. "Maybe," he said. "But I had a feeling this man knew me and I knew him. He was desperately afraid I'd get close enough to recognize him."

"That would be the reaction of any thief. It's up to you, but I suggest that we don't bother Carl Sebold with this, since no harm was done. He has more serious problems on his mind."

"But shouldn't we post a guard on these tents? There are thousands of dollars worth of gear stored here."

"I'm responsible for equipment. You leave it to me. If Mr. Lightfingers comes back he'll get the surprise of his life."

"All right, Dr. Malloy," Jerry said doubtfully. "We'll do it your way."

Later, as he crawled into bed, he tried to sort out the events of the evening. Malloy's explanation was probably right: some poor hungry villager trying to steal a bit of food. But if that were true, why had the man doubled back down the creek toward camp and run the chance of being caught? It was puzzling. And strangest of all was Tom Malloy's suggestion that they keep the incident to themselves.

CHAPTER 7

J ERRY's ankle was swollen and sore next day but by favoring
his left leg he could get about fairly well. He avoided Dr.
Baimbridge because he was afraid the doctor might notice
his limp and order him to bed. But he could hide nothing from
Rick, who demanded to know what had happened. Rick listened to the account without comment. Shortly afterward he
left camp alone and climbed up to the village.

When he returned that evening, he told Jerry he had learned
nothing about the mysterious prowler. The people of Terang
were poor, to be sure, but they had a stern tabu against steal-
ing. In times past serious offenders had had their right hands
amputated for punishment. Theft was practically unknown.

76

Still, a daring and desperate man might be tempted to steal from what he looked upon as rich American *sahibs*.

"I think Malloy is right not to tell Dr. Sebold," he said. "But for the wrong reason."

"What's your reason?"

"By keeping this quiet we'll have a better chance to catch the man."

"Rishkesh Dawa, Private Eye."

Rick grinned. "One of these days you'll see. There's something fishy going on. I can smell it. But I can't put my finger on it."

Early the following morning the expedition got under way, all but Johansen and two Nepalis, who were to tend base camp. The extra days of rest had revived everyone and they climbed well. By nightfall they were camped once more beside the lake, within sight of Yeti Pass. During their absence the snowpack had hardened and the weather promised to hold fair.

At dawn half the porters started down again for a second load of supplies, while Dr. Sebold divided the remainder of his group into four-man teams and laid out their search patterns. Jerry drew Ross Howe, Dorje, the head bearer, and Ang Nuri, the Sherpa from Sikkim, a combination which pleased him. Dorje was the number one climber and Ang the only Sherpa who spoke English, which might be useful.

The weakest member, he admitted, was himself. His ankle, although tightly taped, still bothered him. But he said nothing, determined not to be left behind in camp.

Dr. Sebold held a final briefing. "The main thing to remember," he cautioned them, "is not to push too hard and fast.

We're a long way from help if anything goes wrong. Cover the ground but leave yourselves a margin of safety. That goes double for you, Tom."

Malloy shrugged.

"We'll keep in contact as much as possible, so we can co-ordinate the hunt. These walkie-talkies send and receive a long way under ideal conditions."

"If I meet a fifteen-foot man-eating *yalmo*," Rick said, "I won't need a radio. They'll hear me hollering clear down in Katmandu."

Everybody laughed. "Good luck, gang," Dr. Sebold said. "We'll meet back here in five days. No later."

The three teams separated and moved out on their assigned routes. Jerry and Howe, with the two Sherpas, climbed slowly the first day. Howe was thorough and tireless. At noon he gave the team an hour's rest and pushed on, inspecting every likely draw and hummock. They crossed from snow to rock and back to snow, but found no trace of yetis. Late in the afternoon he called a halt, chose a campsite in a hollow below the pass, and they pitched their two tiny tents.

At six o'clock Malloy's team, camped on a ridge several miles to their left, reported by radio that no yeti tracks had been sighted.

From experience Jerry knew that without a pressure cooker it took hours to boil a single potato. At this altitude a cooker was as vital as boots and snow goggles. He and Dorje set up the primus stove, melted snow, and prepared the favorite Sherpa dish of *mo-mo*, a delicious soup of flour and meat balls. For a beverage they drank a concoction of hot sweet lemon juice, a better thirst-quencher than water or tea.

There were many such techniques climbers over the years had learned about survival on the high peaks, Howe told him. For instance, to eat snow only made a man thirstier. It was better to sleep with your boots on, otherwise they might be frozen stiff by morning. The greatest danger of all, when a man grew careless, was fatigue from lack of oxygen. More climbers died of exhaustion than from avalanches or storms or accidents.

Jerry nodded, trying to listen attentively, and fell asleep.

Before daylight Howe routed him out. They decided to leave the camp set up and return that night. With only light packs they labored up the pass and onto the summit, stopping beside a mound of stones. From it rose a pole, on the end of which a tattered rag fluttered in the wind. Dorje and Ang placed pebbles on the pile and walked around it in a circle.

"That's a prayer flag," Howe said. "A shrine, to these people. They're asking for good luck."

Jerry peered at an inscription on one of the rocks. "What's that say?"

"It's the Tibetan prayer, *Om mane padme om.* 'Sacred Jewel in the lotus.' Not many Tibetans travel this way nowadays, since the Reds took over."

Howe got out his aneroid and determined their elevation to be almost eighteen thousand feet, the highest Jerry had ever been. Then they spread out over the snow, but a half hour search turned up neither footprints nor animal droppings of any kind. If yetis had passed here they had left no sign.

The view was disappointing. A higher ridge rose above them, cutting off the country beyond. Howe unfolded his map while Jerry studied the terrain through binoculars. "A map's not much use here," Howe said. "Most of this country is still unsurveyed. But from that next ridge we might get a pretty fair idea of what's beyond."

Ang Nuri pointed to the ridge. "Is bad place," he said.

"Why? What's wrong with it?"

"Is no good place, *sahib*."

"How do you know, Ang? Have you ever been there?" Howe asked.

Ang shook his head. "Better not to go. Bad place."

"Nonsense. Let's go have a look. We need all the information we can gather."

With obvious reluctance Ang followed the others down off the pass. Aside to Jerry, Howe said, "That Sikkim fellow is actually afraid of something. I wonder what."

"Probably some superstition."

A dim trail led down the slope into a narrow valley. No vegetation grew there and great brown boulders thrust out of the snow. It was a bleak, lonely spot, surrounded by ridges, with only the sound of wind to relieve the silence. It looked lifeless, as if no creature had ever set foot on its forbidding soil, and Jerry could understand why a man like Ang Nuri might feel uneasy.

The trail twisted and turned through the rocks and abruptly came out into a flat, open space. His heart leaped into his throat. Two huge black and white birds which had been feeding flapped their wings and flew away, clumsily at first, as their heavy bodies lifted into the air, and then with effortless grace as they gained height. Shading his eyes against the sun, he watched the two lammergeiers dwindle to specks in the sky.

"Looks like we interrupted their feast," Howe said. "What carrion do you suppose they found?"

Among the rocks he discovered a yak skull with long curved horns, part of a rib cage and a few bones, all picked clean of hide and meat. Vultures had carried off the rest. Scattered beside the trail were the embers of an old fire. "This must be Nemi's yak," Jerry said.

"It sure didn't wander up here. No grass. Somebody drove it over the pass."

"Look!" Jerry picked up one of the rib bones and poked his finger through a neat round hole. "Bullet hole. This yak was shot."

Howe inspected the bone and then bent over the ring of fire-blackened rocks. Presently he straightened with a fragment of charred bone. "And the same somebody cooked himself some meat. Several somebodies is my guess. One yak would feed a lot of men."

He turned suddenly to Ang. "Is this what you were afraid of, Ang?"

Ang's face was pale. "Ang tell you this bad place, Howe *sahib*. Better go back."

"Ask Dorje what he makes of this bone."

The two Sherpas talked excitedly for several minutes. Then Ang translated. "Dorje say no Sherpa kill. He not know how yak come here."

Howe exchanged a look with Jerry. "This happened weeks ago, before we left New York."

"John Conrad was in Terang then," Jerry said. "He might be able to explain it."

"We'll ask him when we get back. But right now—" Howe began to search again, pawing through the snow and over-turning rocks.

It was Jerry who, several minutes later, found the vital clue. In a crack between two boulders he spied some small gray object, and fished out a crumpled cigarette pack. For a second the printing on it puzzled him, then he recalled the warning of the old lama at Terang Gompa. "Dr. Howe!"

Howe frowned at the pack and gave a low whistle. "Chinese! That's it! Of course."

"You think it was a military patrol?"

"Couldn't have been anything else. Slipped across the border into Nepal territory. They wouldn't scruple at driving off a stray yak and butchering it for dinner. Nobody's been up here since."

"But what were *they* doing here?"

"They weren't looking for yetis," Howe said grimly.

Jerry felt a chill chase down his backbone, as he peered around the silent, empty valley. He had read about Chinese Reds, and heard about them. Until now they had seemed re-mote and unreal. But suddenly they began to take on substance in his imagination. They could be, might very well be, around the next bend of the trail, behind the next hill.

"By thunder!" Howe exclaimed. "I've got to climb that ridge now. I want a peek at the other side."

"How far to the frontier?"

Howe glanced at his map. "Several miles beeline, as near as I can figure. Twice as far on foot. How about it, Ang? Are you and Dorje game?"

Dorje agreed at once. Ang, after some persuasion, gave in, although with much muttering. They shouldered their packs and started off again.

The trail swung west up the valley floor, but Howe turned aside through another maze of boulders and climbed steadily toward the ridge crest. Jerry's ankle throbbed a little but he had no difficulty keeping up. Shortly they came to a steep snow slope and separated to look for an easier route around it.

Howe came back shaking his head. "Looks tougher than I thought. Have you ever climbed on a rope, Jerry?"

"No, sir."

"Maybe you'd better wait down here for us."

"I can make it."

Howe gave him a searching look. "This won't be any picnic. Sure you feel up to it?"

"I feel fine."

"Come on then." They put on their crampons and Howe took a coil of rope from his pack and tied a double loop about his waist. He paid out about thirty feet, knotted another loop around Jerry's chest, and did the same for the Sherpas. "Make sure one foot is firm before you move the other, keep looking up, not down. And if you slip, don't panic. There are three of us in support."

Dorje took the lead, moving with sure-footed ease, followed by Ang, then Jerry, with Howe in the rear as anchor man. For the first few hundred yards the ascent was not hard. Then they came to ice. Although it looked treacherous to Jerry, the Sherpas didn't hesitate.

Ang drove the point of his axe into the ice and looped the

rope about the stock to belay Dorje. Secured in this way, Dorje inched up and chopped a step, then another, and another, until he had cut a dozen or so. While he paused to rest the other three climbers moved up behind him one at a time, using the same footholds. It was slow work, but by repeating the process again and again they gradually neared the summit.

The most difficult stretch was a slick, narrow ledge some twenty feet across. Below the mountain dropped off sheer. Dorje and Ang scampered across like goats. Now it was Jerry's turn. He clenched his jaw. Behind him Howe said, "Steady. We're almost there."

He drew a deep breath into his lungs and edged ahead. Dorje turned, belaying on the rope, and smiled reassuringly and motioned him on. His spikes bit into the ice. For an instant he felt paralyzed with fright. He could not move forward or back. Why hadn't he taken Howe's advice and waited below? Then he found his balance and new confidence surged into him.

Crossing the ledge on steady legs, he stepped out on a broad shelf beside the Sherpas. A minute later Howe joined them, and they climbed up a final rise to the ridge crest.

This view was staggering. Peak after peak marched across the northern horizon in a stupendous wall. For a long time no one spoke, as they drank in the mighty spectacle. Then Howe pointed. "That's Gauri Sankar, never been climbed. Some experts claim it never can be."

"They said that about Everest until a few years ago," Jerry remarked.

"One by one the giants fall. There aren't many 'firsts' left." Howe sighed and got out his binoculars again. "But we're not here to climb mountains."

The country below the ridge appeared to be as empty as the valley through which they had just passed. There was no sign of life, no visible trail, no indication that the Chinese had traveled it recently. Maybe, Jerry said, they had lost their way and blundered across the frontier by mistake. It would be easy to do in this wild, uninhabited region.

But Howe had a different opinion. He believed the Reds had come deliberately, to learn if the Nepalis had any soldiers or fortifications in the area. And since they had gotten away with it once, they might be bolder now and come again.

"You may be right at that," he said to Ang. "This isn't a healthy spot for peaceful yeti hunters."

"They make plenty trouble."

"Have you ever seen any in Sikkim, Ang?"

"Oh, yes, sometime they come. Very bad people. Do bad things." Ang scowled. "Ready we go back now, *sahib?*"

"I guess we've seen all there is." Howe put a hand on Jerry's shoulder. "You did fine on the way up. Slow and easy does it. We're not out to break any speed records."

They roped on again and started back down the ridge in the same order, with Jerry in third position. Before they had gone far he knew that his calf and leg and thigh muscles were more tired than he'd realized. They ached with weariness. And pain shot through his ankle with every step. Also, he had to look *down* now. He could see the dizzy gulfs of space that yawned beneath his boots. The rocks far below seemed to be waiting for him to make one mistake, one tiny slip.

By the time they worked across the ledge his knees were trembling. Sweat soaked his clothes. And once more they came to the steep ice slope.

The sun, beating down out of a cloudless afternoon sky, had melted the steps. They felt soft and mushy. He wanted to shut his eyes. But now, more than ever, he had to watch his footing. Step-kick-down. Step-kick-down. His eyes behind their goggles watered from the constant dazzling snow glare. Vapor from his breathing fogged the lenses. Step-kick-down—

Somehow it happened. Maybe he hurried. Maybe he took his eyes off the step ahead. Maybe a puff of wind caught him. But something made his right foot slip. To recover his balance he brought his left foot down hard, driving his spikes into the ice. Hot pain jabbed his ankle and it crumpled under him like rubber.

He yelled. Then he was slipping and sliding, frantically struggling to dig in his axe, but his momentum tore it from his grasp. He clawed for a grip with his gloved hands and both feet shot out from under him.

He seemed to drop forever, hurtling into space. Then the rope tightened under his arms with a terrific jerk. He spun about and came to a stop against the ice face, dangling in his harness, barely able to breathe. He could not move or think. He was too numb.

"Jerry!" Howe shouted down. "Are you all right?"

He raised his eyes. Howe and Dorje had him belayed from their axe poles on the slope above. Their feet were braced and he could see the strain of his weight on their faces. Ang was peering down at him, measuring the distance. If any one of them slipped now, all four would go plunging over.

"Hold tight! We'll get you up." The rocks swirled crazily. The rope burned his chest. He felt helpless, faint, as if at any second he might black out and fall all the way.

Snap out of it, Dunham. Keep your head.

"Can you find a foothold?" Howe panted.

He shifted one foot. It was like treading air. He groped left and right, stretching his legs. His toe felt a niche that gave him some support, and he inched his body over. Face pressed against the ice, he clung there.

"Good boy!"

He heard the crunch of an axe and particles of ice showered down. Risking another upward glance, he saw Ang. With one hand the Sherpa clutched a rope, with the other he was chopping steps. Metal flashed in the sun. Ice chips flew. One step. Two. Three. Then Ang stopped, drove a piton into the ice and ran his rope through the eyelet.

As agile as a monkey, he came down the slope. Three more steps. Another piton. Closer, closer. He was beside Jerry now, hacking out a ledge into which he hammered a final piton and secured the rope. He made a circle of his thumb and finger, grinned his gold-toothed grin.

"Come on, young *sahib*. Is safe now."

Jerry stepped over onto the ledge and grabbed the rope. Nothing had ever felt so good as solid ice under his feet. If there had been room he would have sunk to his knees and breathed a prayer. "Thanks, Ang," he gasped.

"Is nothing."

"Nothing! You risked your neck."

"Is my job. I am Sherpa. Everest Tiger."

The little man's voice swelled with pride.

CHAPTER 8

USING an ice axe as a cane, Jerry was able to hobble back over Yeti Pass on his own two feet, but it was dark before they reached their tents in the hollow. He had never been so tired, nor so disgusted with himself. Howe struck a light and insisted on pulling off his boot to examine the injured ankle. When he saw the tape his eyes widened.

Jerry had to tell him how he had twisted it before the expedition left base camp. His fall on the ice had aggravated the old sprain. "You mean you've been limping around on that sore ankle all this time?"

"I know I should have gone to the doctor but I didn't want to stay in camp."

"Can't say I blame you. But that's what you're going to do. Sit in camp until this heals."

Jerry could only nod.

"Another thing." With a pair of scissors from his first-aid kit Howe cut the layers of tape and yanked them off. "At this altitude never tape a leg or an ankle or a foot too tight. It restricts the circulation. Poor circulation brings on frostbite. And usually you never know till too late."

He pulled off his own right boot and sock. Jerry stared. All but the two smallest toes were missing from his foot. "Gangrene," Howe said. "I lost 'em on Makalu. That's what can happen if you don't take care of yourself."

"I pulled a dumb stunt, all right."

"Not dumb, Jerry. What you did took guts. Remember this, though. Never be afraid of a mountain when you climb. But always respect it."

"I'd like to give Ang something."

"He doesn't expect it. That was all part of the day's work. These Sherpas have a proud tradition."

"That's what I can't understand. He was fearless on the ice, but finding the yak carcass really shook him."

"Not all these mountain folk are superstitious," Howe said, "but they lead a simple life, close to nature. Their senses are keener than ours. As my old grandma used to say, 'They have a nose for trouble.' "

"But he knew something," Jerry said. "He wanted to turn back."

"He knew we were close to the frontier. Maybe that's your answer." Howe yawned. "Rub your ankle down with snow. Then turn in. It's been a long day."

The next day was even longer, or so it seemed to Jerry, and the day after that. While Howe and the Sherpas continued the search, he remained behind in camp nursing his ankle. He had nothing to do except eat and sleep or stare at the rocks and snow. Twice a day he tried to get in touch with the other teams, but they had moved out of range. It was a dull wait, but he told himself he had learned his lesson.

The morning of the fifth day Howe gave the order to pack up. Jerry could walk without a stick but found that his ankle still was weak. At a slow pace they made their way back down to the lake camp.

Dr. Sebold's team had arrived already and an hour later Malloy's team tramped in. Their glum faces told the story. Nobody had seen tracks. The hunt had yielded nothing. Unless, Jerry thought, you counted a few yak bones and a bullet hole.

Worse still, he was not to go on the second hunt. Dr. Baimbridge poked and prodded his ankle and said, "Does that hurt?"

"Hardly at all."

"You're not a very good actor, young fellow. You're going down to base camp. Tomorrow."

"But I can walk, doctor!"

"No arguments. It's badly inflamed. Get down out of this snow, or you might suffer some permanent damage. Soak in the sun. Rest. That's the only cure."

Rick tried to cheer him up. "You lucky stiff, Jerry. While we're freezing up here you'll be living in luxury."

He managed to grin. "Sure. Bring me a yeti. Alive and kicking."

Accompanied by two Nepali porters, he made the trip down

to Terang valley in one long day. He knew the doctor was right. All the same he felt low. The Dunham jinx seemed to be working overtime.

Lars Johansen, the botanist, was a friendly, quiet man, and time at base camp passed pleasantly. Wildflowers, at their short seasonal peak, covered the meadow with brilliant pink and blue and yellow blooms. He spent hours teaching Jerry how to identify the different species.

Now and then men came from the village, bringing rodents and other small animals they had trapped for the expedition. For each specimen Jerry paid one rupee, the price agreed upon. By now he was familiar with most of the local mammals, and he kept busy skinning and classifying each day's bag. Eventually they would be shipped to America, mounted, and presented to various natural history museums for exhibit.

It chafed him to be confined to camp, but he followed the doctor's orders faithfully. Nothing was going to keep him from the next hunt.

One night a strange noise woke him. Usually a sound sleeper, he sat up in bed and listened. He was used to the moan of the wind and the rumble of falling ice up on the glacier. But this had come from somewhere nearby. Probably a boulder turning in the creek, he thought. Or one of the Nepalis talking in his sleep.

The village dogs, half a mile distant, set up a clamor, yapping and baying frenziedly. They were ferocious Tibetan mastiffs, he knew, whose masters kept them chained at night. So it must have been something else. Then he heard the sound again, very close now, a deep angry cough that made his scalp prickle.

Grabbing his flashlight, he dashed outside. Johansen burst out of the next tent in his pajamas at the same moment. "What was that?"

"Sounded like some animal."

The Nepalis came running, chattering with excitement. Everybody had heard the sound. And everybody had a different explanation. With flashlights and lanterns they searched the camp and found nothing. Gradually the racket of the dogs subsided to an occasional howl. Apparently their visitor had slunk away in the dark.

Jerry checked the supply tents, but their flaps were laced up tight. "Has anybody been in these tents since we left?" he asked Johansen.

"No. Tom Malloy gave me strict orders to keep the men out."

"Could that have been a man we heard? Some prowler?"

"Not anybody from Terang," Johansen said. "The dogs caught the scent. They wouldn't bark like that at a villager they knew."

Finally they all went back to bed, but it was some time before Jerry fell asleep. The prowler two weeks ago had been a man. The dogs hadn't barked then. Maybe the wind had been wrong. Or maybe— Did yetis have a scent that would carry half a mile? All sorts of wild possibilities floated through his mind.

It seemed as if he had barely closed his eyes when somebody was shaking him. He blinked up at Johansen. "Pile out, boy! We've found our snooper."

Jerry threw on his clothes and stamped out into a gray dawn.

A crowd of excited Sherpas from the village was pouring into camp. Some led dogs on ropes. Others carried ancient rifles and aiming forks slung across their shoulders.

"This is the *shikar*." Johansen indicated a man with a scarred face. "The village hunter. He's the one who tracked the bear."

"Bear?"

"A big one, the *shikar* says. Killed a yak last night, then took off into the woods. We're going after it now."

Johansen popped back into his tent and reappeared with the big game rifle and a box of shells. "Their old smooth bore muskets don't pack much firepower, so they asked me to shoot it." He loaded the magazine. "Grab your camera, Jerry, and come along."

He looked from the hunter's scarred face off toward the dark line of trees at the lower end of the valley. Balu Kosi. Bear River. Bear country. Rough country, too, full of boulders, deadfalls, dense brush, and tangled vines. He longed to go. Surely his ankle had healed enough by now.

But the doctor's orders had been emphatic: stay close to camp and keep off the ankle as much as possible. Jerry swallowed his disappointment and said, "Guess I'd better not. I'd slow you down too much."

"Well, hold down the fort."

With a wave of his hand Johansen strode off, followed by the Nepalis. The Sherpas fanned out into a line of beaters, shouting, pounding on drums, with their dogs snarling and snapping at the leash. Women, children, in fact most of Terang village, trotted along behind, eager to be in on the kill of this feared and hated enemy. Jerry watched them advance across the meadow and disappear into the undergrowth. After a bit their tumult died away, and he was alone beside the creek.

He walked over to the rock-wall enclosure where the livestock was penned at night. The yak carcass, cruelly mauled, lay on the bloodstained grass. In its fury the bear had ripped and torn the sod for yards around. He studied the huge prints, trying to read their story.

Evidently the bear had climbed the wall, lunged across the pen, and broken the yak's neck with one mighty swipe of its paw. It had not eaten much. Probably the dogs had frightened it off, still raging hungry. But the tracks of this bear, he decided, were not like those of the yeti in the snow. They could not be one and the same creature.

He returned to camp, warmed coffee, and set to work skinning two marmots that he hadn't finished the day before. From time to time he glanced down the valley, but the hunters were out of sight and sound. He got out his drying boards, pinned on the skins, and set them in the shade. It was so quiet and peaceful that he dozed off.

He thought of his parents, halfway around the world, and of Mr. Trevor, who had made all this possible. He thought of Zoology II Lab. But his thoughts kept swinging back to the teams up at the lake camp. Had they been successful this time, or chalked up another failure? Would the expedition ever find a yeti?

A hoarse grunt jarred him out of his reverie. He jumped to his feet. A great brown bear was lumbering up the creek bank toward camp.

The animal paused, shook himself, and raised his snout, sniffing the wind. Underneath the shaggy mud-spattered coat he looked gaunt, half-starved, as if he had found little feed in the high mountains. Jerry identified him instantly as the dreaded Tibetan red bear, the grizzly of the Himalayas. Either he had eluded the hunters and doubled back upon his tracks, or this was the mate.

He had been running. His flanks were heaving from exertion. Now he turned his head and peered back over one shoulder toward the forest, as though to make sure he had shaken off all pursuit. Apparently satisfied, the beast stood swaying from side to side and directed his attention back to camp once more. Jerry licked his lips and stared at the piglike eyes, at the hooked claws which curved from the forepaws like small black daggers.

Most bears had poor eyesight. They depended on their sense of smell. They could move with tremendous speed over a short distance. He knew that much. And they seldom attacked man unless they were cornered or desperately hungry. If he stood absolutely still the beast might ignore him and go on his way.

But he had forgotten the two marmot skins. The beast caught the smell of fresh blood. With a snort he started forward, massive shoulders rolling. Cautiously he approached the pile of entrails, swallowed them up in one gulp, and batted the drying boards aside. Ten yards away, Jerry held his ground. His heart hammered. He could hardly breathe. But he could smell the bear now. It was a rank, musky, almost overpowering stench.

The bear blinked in his direction. He snuffled and sniffed

the ground and his manner said plainly: "That was only an appetizer. I want more." The huge blunt head lifted. The mouth opened, revealing yellow fangs. Jerry froze. Then another scent diverted the bear. He whirled about and shambled into the mess tent.

The canvas sides bulged. There was a crash of cans and mess kits and the stove overturned with a clatter. Cloth ripped and pots clanged, and the tent shook as if a tornado had struck it. Jerry looked about wildly. Surely the hunters must turn back soon. Would they hear him if he yelled?

In his ravening search for food the bear might demolish every tent, smash irreplaceable equipment and supplies. Jerry had seen grizzlies paw the garbage dumps at Yellowstone Park, but never anything like this. Johansen had taken the rifle. There was not another weapon in camp. Then he remembered the knockout gun. Malloy hadn't carried the gas rifle up to the lake camp on his back.

He raced to the tent that Malloy and Dr. Sebold shared, and made a frantic search. On his knees he fumbled under the cots. It had to be there! His fingers touched leather and he pulled out the rifle case. Then the metal tackle box. Now if he could only make it work.

He had seen Malloy operate the rifle, but he had forgotten the drug formula. What was the dosage? A milligram for each three pounds of weight? That bear must weigh at least five hundred pounds. He'd have to guess and make it strong. With shaking hands he mixed the solution and poured it into a syringe, fastened on a needle dart, and fitted it into the rifle, then inserted a carbon dioxide cylinder.

One shot, he thought. One dart. It seemed impossible that this gadget could stop a quarter ton of maddened brute. Like aiming a peashooter at an elephant. And if he missed there wouldn't be time to reload.

The uproar in the mess tent ceased abruptly. As he stepped forward the bear charged out and reared to his hind legs. Jerry swallowed. Towering above him, the beast looked enormous, pawing at his face, which was white with sugar from the cook stores. He felt like a pygmy as he raised the rifle to his shoulder and cocked the hammer.

He sighted along the barrel and squeezed the trigger. There was a sharp "thock." The bear growled deep in his throat, weaving and bobbing like some huge hairy boxer. Jerry stood paralyzed, uncertain whether he had hit a vein, a layer of fat or missed altogether. If it took the drug four minutes to work— Then he heard the distant barking of dogs and a faint shout. The hunters! They were coming.

He dared not look away. With a roar the bear dropped back on all fours, sensing danger from another quarter. He raked the ground and sank back on his haunches. Then, to Jerry's disbelief, he slowly toppled on his side and with a final twitch collapsed.

The rifle dropped from Jerry's fingers. He wiped his dripping face on his sleeve. On limp, shaky legs he stepped closer. The bear stirred, breathing heavily, and lay still.

Minutes later Lars Johansen, his face a fiery red, puffed into camp, followed by a swarm of villagers. When they saw the bear a yell of triumph went up and the dogs leaped about in a frenzy. "I'll be!" Johansen exploded. "The brute slipped past us somehow. I never dreamed he'd show up here." His eyes widened as he took in the wreckage of the mess tent. "How did you—"

"Malloy's knockout gun," Jerry said. "He's alive."

"Alive?" Johansen peered over the heads of the crowd, which had gathered around the bear at a respectful distance. "Beautiful specimen. Shame to kill him."

"Do we have to?"

Johansen rubbed his jaw. "How soon will the dope start wearing off?"

"Fifteen minutes or less."

"We'll have to work fast." Johansen turned to the *shikar* and spoke a few phrases. The *shikar* nodded and grinned broadly and the crowd broke into an excited buzz. Half a dozen men ran toward the trees. "They're going to make a cage."

"You mean we can keep him?"

"Why not? He's your bear. That's the rule of the hunt these people live by." Johansen slapped him on the shoulder. "Not a bad morning's work. Next to a yeti, I'd say you bagged the number one prize. Right in camp."

"I hate to think where I might be now if I'd missed."

"Better give Sleeping Beauty another shot of tranquilizer. We don't want him waking up till we're ready."

While the admiring crowd looked on, Jerry filled another syringe and reloaded the rifle. He had to fire a second and third dart into the bear to keep him quiet, but in less than an hour the Sherpas put together a cage of hardwood poles they had cut hastily in the forest. Under the *shikar's* direction they tied ropes around the bear's forepaws and pulled his hulk into the cage. The cage was crude but strong, with a sliding panel at one end secured by leather thongs and a small opening for food and water.

As a final touch Johansen painted a sign, which he nailed to the door: "BIG RED, *Ursus arctos isabellinus*, captured by Jerry Dunham and presented to this zoo."

Presently Big Red came to. Surrounded by a breathless audience, he rolled over and got to his feet. He growled and snapped a little, sniffed at the bars, turned around a time or two as though inspecting his new quarters, then slumped down, and went to sleep. With the dusting of sugar still on his snout he looked almost comic. Jerry could hardly believe it was the same animal.

"Well-behaved guest now, isn't he," Johansen said.

"He has a full belly, that's why. He ate about fifty pounds of our sugar."

"We'll have to give another feast."

"For the hunters?"

"For the whole village. They were counting on that bear meat. The least we can do is feed them."

"*All* of them?"

"That's only a hundred people or so." Johansen grinned. "Put on your chef's cap and go to work."

The celebration got under way at sundown. The villagers brought bowls of *chang*, the local beer, and the lamas brought gifts of barley cakes. They consumed immense quantities of mulligan stew which Jerry had spent the afternoon preparing. When everyone had eaten his fill the musicians produced their horns and drums and the dance began, a weird shuffling step with men, women, and children linking arms and chanting to the rhythm. By the light of flickering torches Jerry and Johansen looked on.

"They've composed a song in your honor," Johansen said. "I don't understand all the words, but it's about the mighty *sahib* who slew the dreaded bear."

"I didn't slay him."

"Poetic license. It sounds better. You're the hero of Terang village tonight."

"Some hero." Jerry laughed. "I was too scared to run."

He walked over to the cage for a last look before turning in for the night. The bear shifted in his sleep and twitched an ear. One of these days he would be carried down the steep mountain trails to Katmandu, transferred to a steel cage, and flown over the oceans to America. There, in some zoo, he would live out his final days.

"Tough luck, Red," Jerry said. "But don't complain. You almost ended up in the stewpot."

CHAPTER 9

THE other members of the expedition returned the following afternoon. Jerry didn't have to ask what success they'd had. The men were tired and dirty and silent as they filed into camp. For weeks they had been living and working at high altitudes and the strain showed on every face.

But they brightened at the sight of the bear and crowded around the cage. Jerry had to retell the story of Big Red's capture and answer endless questions. Their congratulations embarrassed him. Thanks to a sore ankle he had been in the right place at the right time. It was one of those crazy, lucky breaks that sometimes happened.

"It's one of the world's rarest bears," Dr. Sebold said. "Only a few in captivity."

"How about that?" Malloy said. "Not many natives have ever seen one. So this one walks smack into Dunham's arms."

Howe winked at Jerry. "What were you saying about a jinx?"

"Maybe we should all sprain our ankles," Rick said. "Jerry has the best system."

"Mr. Trevor will be tickled, Jerry," Dr. Sebold said. "If we never see another yeti track, we'll not be going home empty-handed."

But yetis remained the expedition's number one mission. Next evening, after the men had enjoyed a twenty-four-hour rest, he called them together. They had to expect certain set-backs and disappointments, he said. Actually they should be pleased with results so far. They had cleared up several mis-conceptions about the creature and eliminated one large area of their search, besides collecting a number of valuable speci-mens.

But the short mountain summer was passing. They might expect rains soon, and once autumn closed in on them with heavy snow and ice conditions, operations at higher eleva-tions would become almost impossible. This left time for two more major hunts before returning to Katmandu.

The discussion went on late into the night. Ross Howe favored striking northeast toward the approaches of Mount Everest. John Conrad proposed a wide circle to the west. Tom Malloy had still another idea. And so it went. No two members could agree where their chances might be best. Fi-nally Dr. Sebold turned to Jerry. "Let's hear from the bear hunter. You haven't said a word."

"Well," he began, "we might find yetis in any one of these places. But it seems to me we're overlooking one possibility right under our noses."

"What's that, Jerry?"

"The villagers. They're out in the mountains every day herding yaks, collecting wood, hunting herbs and game. Altogether they spread over a lot of country."

"They know we're looking for yetis. They'll be the first to tell us," Malloy interrupted.

"Yes, but—" Jerry hesitated as he saw the impatient frown on Malloy's face. Then, encouraged by Dr. Sebold's nod, he went on. "If they do find anything it will be pure luck. Like Nemi with his missing yak. They're all scared of yetis anyway. But if we offer a reward, say a hundred rupees, they'll really turn out. They'll cover the map for us."

"It's worth a try," Dr. Sebold said. "We can't lose anything."

The men were still arguing when Jerry slipped off to the mess tent to make a pot of coffee. He had cleaned up the shambles left by the bear two days before, but some of the pots bore the scars of Big Red's fury. He struck a match and turned on the stove burner, but after a moment or two the flame hissed out. The fuel tank was empty. He remembered then that Big Red had ripped open the extra five-gallon fuel container they kept on hand, spilling gas over the floor. He would have to get another can from the first supply tent.

Usually one of the Sherpas took care of the stove but they were all asleep at this hour. He walked down the row to the big end tent beside the creek. He hadn't been inside since the night of the prowler. No one had, except possibly Malloy. He loosened the knots which held down the flap and flipped it back and stepped through the opening.

Before he could switch on his flashlight his ankle collided with something. He tripped and sprawled forward, striking his head on a box. There was a terrific clatter of metal objects falling all around him. He tried to jump up and tripped again, setting off another racket.

Men were running and shouting outside and he saw the gleam of lights as they neared the tent. A torch flashed in his eyes and he blinked at the muzzle of a rifle not ten feet before his face.

"Good grief, it's you, Jerry!" Dr. Sebold poked his head in. "I thought the bear had broken loose."

He sat up and rubbed his head. His feet were tangled in rope. Empty cans were scattered over the floor.

"What happened?"

"I'm not sure. I came in to get some stove fuel and—bingo!"

"Looks like some kind of a booby trap," Rick said. He bent down and examined the cans.

Dr. Sebold helped Jerry to his feet. He wasn't hurt, only dazed. A babble of excited voices, in Sherpa and Nepalese as well as English, rose outside the tent. He had wakened the whole camp. And probably the whole village, too, he thought, with that racket.

"Look." Rick pointed to a length of rope stretched taut at ankle height between two stakes just inside the entrance. "That's what you tripped over."

Jerry stared. Every can had been punctured and tied to

the rope with a piece of string. Anyone who entered in the dark as he had, unsuspecting, would bring them crashing down around his ears.

Then Malloy came pushing through the crowd. In an embarrassed voice he said, "I guess I'm guilty, Carl. I forgot to tell Dunham about my burglar alarm."

"Burglar alarm? What in the deuce are you talking about, Tom?"

"Dunham thought he saw a snooper around here the other night. So I rigged up this contraption. The idea was to scare off any villager who might get itchy fingers. It backfired, and I'm sorry."

Jerry took a deep breath. He was angry, because Malloy had been so careless and forgetful. Somebody could have been hurt. But he decided not to make an issue of the incident. There was too much bad feeling between them already. He forced a smile and said, "That's okay. But next time try flypaper. It's not so noisy."

When the excitement had died down, the bearers went back to their blankets and the *sahibs* returned to their separate tents, coffee forgotten, without having settled any future plans. For a while Jerry and Rick lay in their bags, talking in low voices.

"That fish smell," Rick said, "is getting fishier."

"Now what?"

"Malloy knew you were the only person likely to go in the supply tent. I think he 'forgot' to tell you about his booby trap accidentally on purpose."

"Just to give me a bump on the head? Rick, that's kid stuff."

"Sure it is. But he's jealous."

Jerry snorted. "Tom Malloy, jealous of me! Why?"

"You should've seen his face when you told us about bagging the bear. With *his* pet rifle. He was green with envy."

"Dream on, Sherlock. But let me get to sleep."

They rose early next morning and climbed to the village and located the house of the *shikar*. When Rick told him of the offer of one hundred rupees to anyone who found yeti tracks, the hunter's eyes brightened. Yes, it was a splendid idea, he agreed. With such an incentive his people would look very hard. They would scour the mountains. If a yeti came anywhere near Terang it surely would be found.

He bustled off to spread the news while Jerry and Rick returned to camp. It was a clear, crisp day and the snow peaks loomed on the horizon. Jerry felt like whistling as they strode across the meadow. He could see Big Red pacing in his cage. Today, he thought, I'll feed Red some more of that yak meat and change his water. Have to keep him healthy.

Then Dr. Sebold and Malloy stepped out from the tents. Their faces were grim. Trouble. More trouble. He was sure of it.

"Jerry," Dr. Sebold said, "the rifle is missing. Tom's knockout gun."

"Missing? Since when?"

"That's what we'd like to know," Malloy said. "You were the last one to use it." He had left the rifle behind in base camp, he explained, because it seemed pointless to carry any extra equipment higher until they were sure of yetis in the area. He had stowed it in its case under his cot. This morning he had decided to clean it. When he looked the tackle box was there, but not the rifle and case.

"When did you see it last?"

"Over two weeks ago, before we moved up to the lake camp."

"I put it back under your cot where I found it," Jerry said. "Three days ago. I haven't touched it since."

"Like you put back that yeti skin?"

Jerry flushed. "Are you calling me a liar, Dr. Malloy?"

"Cool off, you two!" Dr. Sebold said sharply. "Nobody's accusing you. Jerry, exactly what happened after you shot the bear?"

Step by step he described what he had done that day after Big Red collapsed in front of the mess tent. Every detail was clear in his mind. He had picked up the rifle from the ground. Later he had fired a second and third dart into the animal to keep it quiet, while the awe-struck throng of villagers looked on. Finally, he had returned the rifle to Malloy's tent.

"That's right." Lars Johansen, who had joined the group, spoke up. "I saw him myself. Jerry put that rifle back."

"It didn't walk off by itself," Malloy said.

Jerry felt sick, as he had that morning in New York. Once again Malloy suspected him of negligence, or worse. In Malloy's eyes whatever he did was wrong.

"Let's make sure first that it wasn't just mislaid," Dr. Sebold said.

One by one they questioned the Sherpa and Nepali bearers. All denied having seen the rifle or knowing anything about it.

Then they searched the camp from end to end, through every tent, every box and bag large enough to hold the assembled rifle or its parts, and at the end of two hours gave up.

"Are you convinced now, Carl?" Malloy demanded. "Somebody stole it."

"I hate to think so, but it looks that way, since we've had one prowler already. But why didn't the thief take the drug and the syringes and the CO_2 pellets? Without them it's useless."

"I think I can explain that," Howe offered. "These people don't understand how the rifle works. To them it's big magic. Because it knocked out the bear. Probably one of the village hunters couldn't resist the temptation, but didn't realize he needed the other stuff to make it fire."

All the villagers had been in camp the night of the celebration, Jerry recalled. Over a hundred strong, feasting and singing and dancing. In all the noise and confusion anyone could have slipped into Malloy's tent and carried the rifle off in the dark. They had seen him put it there earlier. To some poor native it would have seemed like a symbol of power.

"You should have booby-trapped your own tent, Tom."

"It's no joke," Malloy said. "That rifle was our only chance of taking a yeti alive. So help me, I'll get it back."

"How?"

"How? I'll go over the village with a fine tooth comb."

"Tom, listen to me." Dr. Sebold put a hand on his shoulder. "You're upset by this. We all are. But you can't barge into Terang and accuse every man in sight."

"I'm not letting anybody get away with this."

"You're going to stay right here and simmer down," Dr. Sebold said calmly, "while Rick and I go talk to the *shikar*. We'll ask his help. Those people are our friends and they have a lot of pride. If one of them did steal the rifle, he'll find out."

"For all we know he stole it himself."

"You have to trust somebody. Let's go, Rick."

He and Rick turned up the trail to the village. Malloy looked at Jerry and walked into his tent without another word. "Don't worry, Jerry," Howe said. "They'll clear up this business."

Reassured, Jerry went about his duties. Big Red had been put in his charge, so he refilled the water can and cleaned out the cage. Now that the bear was fed regularly he seemed to accept his new life, almost as if he were tame. Most of the time he slept, head slumped between his great paws, twitching his nose.

The day dragged on. Jerry made entries in the journal. He strung up a new aerial for the radio. Every few minutes he peered up the trail, hoping to see Dr. Sebold and Rick on their way down with the rifle.

But they returned empty-handed. The *shikar*, Dr. Sebold said, had called a meeting of the village elders. To a man they denied any knowledge of the missing rifle. They knew of no strangers who might have taken it. They promised to keep their eyes open, but they were as mystified as the *sahibs*.

"I believe them. And so does Rick."

"Are you dropping it at that?" Malloy asked.

"For the time being. We have more important things to do. But from now on we're going to keep all valuable equipment in the supply tents and post a guard."

Supper was a strained meal that night. There was none of the usual joking and banter. The ugly word "thief" hung in the air, although no one spoke it aloud. And Jerry knew that Malloy held him responsible.

Afterward he copied out the nightly weather broadcast and walked over to Big Red's cage. At the other end of camp a Nepali paced up and down in front of the supply tents. In four hours another guard would relieve him. And so on, around the clock, night and day, until they left the valley for good. Or, unless they caught the thief.

The Sherpa Ang Nuri stepped up beside him and peered through the bars. "Is fine bear, young *sahib*. You like this red one, yes?"

"I wouldn't keep him around the house for a pet."

Ang laughed. "Bear will be famous in America. Many Americans wish to see Tibet bear."

"Yes, he'll go to some zoo," Jerry said.

"Very good. Ang Nuri tell you he bring much luck. Maybe next you find yeti."

"I'd like to find that rifle first."

"Ah? Never find him, I think so."

"Why do you say that, Ang?"

"Is what I feel. Here." The Sherpa tapped his forehead. "Bad thing. Ang know. Never find. Rest well, young *sahib*."

Jerry stared after him thoughtfully. Did Ang know anything about the rifle? No, that was impossible. He had been miles away with the expedition the night it disappeared. Jerry remembered the day on Yeti Pass, when Ang had been so uneasy and warned them not to go on. Like many of these mountain people he seemed to have a sixth sense about such things. His words tonight sounded strangely like a warning, too.

Ang had been worried about Red patrols the other time, and with good reason. But there was no link between them and the rifle, not that Jerry could see. He shook his head as he turned back to his tent. He would never make much of a detective. Leave that to Rick. Now that his ankle had healed all he wanted was to get away from camp and back to the high country.

CHAPTER 10

HE didn't have long to wait. Dr. Sebold called another meeting after breakfast and came straight to the point. "We've pooled all our ideas," he said. "Here's what I've decided. Tom, you and Ross and John are stronger climbers than the rest of us. Take Dorje and two other Sherpas and four Nepalis. Ten in all. Travel fast and light. You're to search, at your discretion, beyond Thyangboche up toward Khumbu Glacier."

Tom Malloy frowned. "Khumbu's not my pick. You know that, Carl. I still think it's a long shot."

"You're outvoted, Tom. We don't have the manpower to do this your way."

"How much time are you giving me?"

They all were conscious of time. This next push might well be the expedition's make-or-break point of no return. A wrong decision would cost them days, when every day was precious.

"Three weeks," Dr. Sebold said. "It's a tight schedule. If you think I'm asking too much—"

"How soon do we leave?"

"As soon as you're ready."

Malloy nodded to Howe and Conrad, who got up and followed him out of the tent. Jerry felt a stab of envy. Khumbu Glacier was the approach to Everest. Malloy's team would traverse the lap of the world's highest peak. But a novice like himself would be an impediment on such a climb.

"Now, gentlemen." With a dry smile Dr. Sebold faced the others. "We seem to be the draft horses of this outfit. Slow but dependable."

Rick's white teeth flashed. "I resent that. Give us a fast track and we'll show that bunch our heels."

"I'm afraid we're in for a slow track this trip." Dr. Sebold jabbed his pipestem at the map. "All reports on the yeti agree on one point. Namely, he avoids man like the plague. Only hunger ever forces him to come near villages or trails or any place contaminated by humans."

"You think we should put out baits?"

"That's been tried. And failed. No, looking for that rifle yesterday, I learned something from the *shikar*. He tells me none of his people have ever been up the Balu Kosi gorge. There's no feed for stock, no game to hunt. It's rough and wild. In fact, it's virgin country, unexplored."

"How about expeditions like ours?"

"No peaks up there to attract climbers. Just a few twenty-thousand-foot dwarfs. Apparently we'll be the first to reach the Balu headwaters—if we make it."

"Sounds like yeti heaven," Dr. Baimbridge said. "Must be a catch though."

"There is. I tried to hire extra bearers. But the villagers won't go near that gorge for any price, poor as they are. Some superstition, I suppose. So we'll have to double up our loads."

Rick gave a mock groan. "My back hurts, coach. Do I have to play?"

Dr. Sebold laughed. "Tomorrow. 5 a.m. Zero hour."

With an air of sober purposefulness they went about their preparations. They packed and repacked, cutting down food and gear to minimum essentials. There would be no stockpiling an advance camp up the Balu Kosi, no reserve dumps to fall back upon. This was a task force stripped to the bone. Even so, each man's load weighed out at close to seventy pounds.

Shivering in the dawn chill next morning, Jerry shouldered his pack and stamped warmth into his feet. A dank mist hovered over the meadow and the two flags, American and Nepalese, hung limp on the flagpole. Sleepy-eyed men straggled into line, blowing on their hands. As they moved off down the trail he glanced back. Three Nepalis had been left behind to guard camp and take care of Big Red. Malloy's team was gone already. Which left—how many?

He counted. Thirteen. Thirteen in Team One. "Are *you* superstitious, Rick?"

"Not me," Rick said. "I never learned to count past twelve."

They descended into the lower valley through the forest, crossed Balu Kosi on the suspension bridge, and turned up the opposite bank. A few clearings, planted in millet, had been hacked out of the trees, but they soon left these behind as they advanced upstream. Gradually the walls closed in until the sky appeared as a narrow slit of blue far above and they were forced to scramble over boulders at the water's edge.

The river was a roaring milky torrent that bathed the canyon bottom in perpetual spray and coated the rocks with mossy slime. For those in boots the footing was treacherous, but the barefoot Nepalis, gripping with their toes, seldom slipped or fell. From time to time they had to wade across the river in waist-deep water, roped together as though on some peak, or fight directly upstream against the battering current. Now and then they came to a gravel bar where they could walk a short distance on level ground before attacking the next obstacle.

To Jerry the gorge became a battleground and the river his relentless enemy. Each step was a fight against exhaustion, a triumph over the dragging weight of his pack and the force of icy water. Sodden clothes hung on him like lead. Shoulder straps sawed into his flesh. Sharp rocks gouged his hands. Head down and jaw set, he slogged on hour after hour.

The canyon grew deeper. Sheer cliffs towered up a thousand feet or more. The river leaped from ledge to ledge, racing down through chutes into wild foaming whirlpools. The Sherpas climbed ahead, drove expansion bolts into the rocks, and rigged a rope over the steepest and most dangerous stretches. To be heard above the boom of the rapids they had to shout. At times he thought they could not possibly advance another yard. But always the Sherpas, urged on by Dr. Sebold, found some crack, some foot- or handhold. Boulder by boulder, pool by pool, bend after bend, they clawed deeper into the unknown.

For three days they struggled up the gorge and then abruptly the cliffs receded and they stumbled out into a barren amphitheater of a valley, surrounded by peaks on three sides. The river led into another canyon mouth but Dr. Sebold gave the order to halt. This was it, he said. Tomorrow they would quit the river and climb to snowline.

While the others were unpacking for the night, Jerry walked upstream to gather firewood. He understood now why the men of Terang had never come to this remote spot. Only crackpot scientists would risk their skins in the gorge of Balu Kosi.

And then he sniffed the acrid odor of burning wood. It was so elusive that he thought he must be mistaken. No one else could be here. But a shift in wind brought the smell to him again, from somewhere upriver. He climbed a few more yards and peered over a rock. From behind a boulder just ahead a faint curl of smoke drifted lazily into the air.

He stared in fascination. The fire, which he could not see, must be man-made. There had been no lightning storms to strike a blaze. Slowly the significance dawned on him. Chinese! A Red patrol! They must have crossed the frontier again and entered this valley from another direction.

His heart racing, he dropped to his knees. He had to warn the others. But first he wanted to see how many soldiers there were, what kind of weapons they carried. He crept forward around the rock and wormed his way up over the big flat-topped boulder. At the edge he raised his head cautiously and peered into the hollow below.

An old man and a boy about ten years old crouched over a tiny fire. They were dark-skinned, like the Sherpas, but they wore fur hats and strange knee-length boots, and their clothes were in rags. On his belt the old man carried a tinderbox and knife and his fingers played over a string of prayer beads as he chanted in a mournful singsong. The longer Jerry stared the more puzzled he became. There were no soldiers or rifles. Only this forlorn and bedraggled pair, here in the middle of nowhere.

The boy suddenly glanced up and caught a glimpse of Jerry. With a cry of alarm he sprang to his feet. The old man dropped his beads and shrank back. "I won't hurt you!" Jerry called.

They stared at him uncomprehendingly with fear on their faces. He climbed down but they backed away and tears welled up in the boy's eyes. Jerry tried his few words of Sherpa, but the old man only shook his head from side to side.

"Maybe you're hungry." He fished a candy bar out of his pocket, peeled off the wrapper, made the sign for eating, and thrust it into the boy's hand.

The boy sniffed the candy suspiciously. His whole body was trembling. Then he took a bite. A shy smile touched his face and he gobbled down the rest.

"That's better. You come along with me."

The old man hesitated and hung back, but at length Jerry conveyed his meaning by gestures. Uncertainly they followed him down the river bank to camp, where their arrival was greeted with amazement.

"Tibetans!" Rick exclaimed in surprise. "Where did *they* come from?"

"I haven't any idea. But I think they're starving."

One of the Sherpas, Tandu, spoke Tibetan. He asked a question, translated the answer into the Sherpa tongue, and Rick translated that into English. "They've been through Hades," Rick said. "Nearly drowned in the river and lost their food. They've been living off bark and roots."

"Tell them we'll share what we have," Dr. Sebold said. "They look done in, poor souls."

"Go easy on the food," Dr. Baimbridge cautioned. "Their systems won't take much at first. Hot tea, a little broth. That's all for tonight."

The boy wolfed down two bowls and fell into an exhausted sleep, but the old man barely touched his soup. In a slow, faltering voice, with many pauses for the interpreters, he told his story.

He was a farmer, he said, and the grandfather of the boy, whose parents had been shot by the Reds. Fearing for the boy's life, he had fled his homeland and escaped with him across the border into Nepal. But they had lost their way in the upper Balu Kosi gorge and wandered for days, until they stumbled into this valley. What happened to him did not matter. He had lived out his span of years. But he wanted the boy to have a chance for a good life in a new land. Would these kind *sahibs*, whom the merciful Lord Buddha had sent like a blessing in this dark hour, help his grandson?

By the time he finished his voice had sunk to a whisper, and the men stared at him with compassion.

"Of course we'll help." Dr. Sebold turned to the doctor. "What shape are they in, Harold?"

"The boy's all right. A little food and rest should do wonders. But the grandpa is suffering from severe malnutrition. That ordeal sapped his strength. He's awfully weak."

"We can't take them with us tomorrow. And we can't leave them here alone."

"I'll stay," Dr. Baimbridge said. "Leave me Tandu. Between us we'll make out."

"I can't ask you to do this, Harold."

"When you're a medico you don't always have a choice." The doctor sighed. "As soon as they're able to travel, Tandu and I'll take them down the river and send word to the authorities."

Jerry looked from one to the other. Another tough decision, he thought. This would split the team and weaken it. But they couldn't abandon a small boy and a feeble, sick old man.

Dr. Sebold nodded in agreement and turned to Rick. "Ask him one more question, if he's not too tired. Did he see any yeti tracks farther up the gorge?"

The old man screwed up his face and pointed toward the cliffs across the river. "No he didn't see tracks," Rick finally translated. "He's never seen any in his life. But—"

"But what?"

"Last night, up there, he heard strange cries, like no animal he ever heard before. He thinks it was a yeti."

Next morning the two groups separated. Team One, reduced to eleven men, said goodbye to the doctor, Tandu, and the two Tibetans. They would not meet again until the return to base camp. With Dr. Sebold in the lead, they forded the river and began to climb.

It was good to escape from the shut-in feeling of the gorge and the eternal roar of water. Fighting the river had been drudgery. Jerry felt a sense of freedom, as if he had broken out from some wet black tunnel into sunlight, and with it a new stir of excitement. The old man's description of cries in the night had been vague, but they might be a clue.

For a week the team searched and crisscrossed back and forth over a region of giant rockslides and snowfields high under the cliffs that hemmed in the Balu Kosi. It was a land that seemed to have a restless life of its own, forever shifting and stirring under the hot sun. Boulders tumbled down without warning. Water from melting snow trickled over every ledge. Rotten, decomposed stone crumbled away under their boots. They took care to avoid old avalanche tracks and fresh rock falls, and at night pitched camp with a wary eye for the heights above.

"I think we'd better turn back tomorrow," Dr. Sebold decided that evening. "I don't like the look of those formations up there."

"Earthquake country, Carl?"

"Could be. But I'm more concerned about the snow pack. With all this dry weather it's turned slushy."

"Do you think the old man really heard anything, Rick?" Johansen asked.

"He thought he did. He was frightened." After a pause Rick added, "Did I ever tell you my favorite yeti story?"

"Is it true?"

"I'll let you judge. Anyway, there was this hunter named Myo who kept hearing yeti calls. He never caught one. They were too smart for him. But he had a theory they were curious creatures, like monkeys, that spied on the villagers and imitated them. So he decided to play a trick.

"One night he gave a party for his friends out in a meadow. They drank *chang* and sang and danced and had a wonderful time. The next night he set out several bowls of *chang* in the same meadow and hid behind a wall to watch. Sure enough, the yetis came out of hiding. They drank up the brew and tried to dance, just like humans. But they weren't used to beer and fell asleep. Myo rushed out and put them all in cages."

"What happened to them?"

"When they woke up they were furious. They smashed the bars and escaped into the mountains. They've never come near a village since."

"The moral being," Dr. Sebold said, "don't count your yetis till they hatch."

They ate their evening meal and sat before their tents in the gathering dusk. Now and then a rock rumbled down the cliffs, its sound magnified in the thin, still air. The men were silent and preoccupied with thoughts of tomorrow. Another failure. Another defeat. And time was running out.

A sudden shrill cry brought them all to their feet. It was an eerie sound that trailed off into a whistle. Then, something like a coyote, the creature began to yelp in quick, explosive barks and ended on a quavering howl that echoed and re-echoed from the cliffs until it died away. In the deep hush that followed Jerry felt gooseflesh prickle his chest.

The Sherpas broke into a shout. "*Kang-mi! Kang-mi!*"

Dr. Sebold held up his hand. "Listen!"

The cry came again from somewhere nearby, then the long piercing whistle and the final howl. Involuntarily Jerry shivered. It was the loneliest, saddest sound he had ever heard.

"Sounds like a cross between a hyena and a loon," Johansen said. "No wonder it scares these people."

Jerry snatched up his binoculars. The light was so dim he could barely distinguish rock from shadow on the slope above. He swept the glasses back and forth, came to rest on a rockslide and sharpened his focus screw a hair's turn. Something dark moved, stopped, moved again and melted into the shadows.

"You spot it, Jerry?"

"Can't be sure. It's gone now."

"Let's go see."

They all raced out of camp across the rocks and up the slope. Panting and puffing, Jerry reached the slide first. He peered up, straining to see any flicker of motion among the shadows. Night was closing in and a cold wind blew off the snow. No sound. Nothing. Then a shower of stones clattered down, as if dislodged by a careless foot.

"Don't go out on that slide," Dr. Sebold said. "Might give way."

"Something's up there. I heard it."

"So did I. Maybe we can corner it under the cliff." Dr. Sebold glanced anxiously at the sky. "Not much light left though."

They climbed up through a pile of boulders, closely followed by Rick, Johansen and the bearers. Nobody wanted to turn back now, despite the darkness. All could plainly hear the clicking scratch of loose rock out on the slide and slightly higher up, as if their quarry were scrambling frantically to keep ahead. Jerry stopped to ease the stitch in his side and catch his breath.

A yeti, he thought. *It has to be a yeti. It can't be anything else. Any second now we'll see it.*

The trickle of loose rock had become a steady rattle. A huge boulder rolled down and bounded past him end over end, and went crashing into the valley below. Then a new noise grew in volume—an ominous grinding rumble. The whole slide seemed to shift and heave like some monster stone serpent suddenly come to life. Horrified, he felt the mountainside tremble under his feet.

One of the Nepalis screamed.

"Down, Jerry! Get down! Avalanche!"

CHAPTER **11**

H<small>E</small> flung himself sideways and covered his head with his arms. The roar of falling rock and snow thundered in his ears. Fragments of flying stone flung off by the avalanche pelted his back. He shut his eyes and prayed, expecting any instant to be crushed and torn away from his perch and swept down the mountain. But gradually the roaring subsided. Once more silence closed over the dusk.

Cautiously he got to his feet, fearful of setting off another slide. A cloud of dust and snow particles boiled over the valley, obscuring the tents. One by one the men crawled out from behind whatever boulder or ledge they had taken cover. Nobody had a thought of resuming the yeti chase. They were thankful to be alive.

"That was close!" Dr. Sebold breathed. "Anybody hurt?"

A quick check revealed that, outside of a nasty scare, all eleven members of the team had come through unharmed. The mass of the avalanche had gone down the slide, miraculously missing them by a few yards. "What started it?" Jerry asked.

"It doesn't take much," Rick said. "Probably just the weight of snow loosened by the day's heat. But if it was a yeti, he's a goner now."

"Look!" Lars Johansen pointed.

Wind had blown away most of the dust. Where camp had stood there was only a gigantic pile of rubble. Their tents, food, sleeping bags, and other gear lay buried under tons of rock and snow. If not for the yeti, they all might have been trapped under the avalanche. And then the chilling thought struck Jerry: in another sense they were trapped, high on a mountain at night, with only the clothes on their backs and miles from help.

"Maybe we can dig out."

"Not tonight. We'll have to wait till tomorrow."

They spent a freezing night huddled together for warmth among the rocks. At the first crack of dawn they climbed down to camp. One close look in daylight at the scene of awesome devastation told them it would be futile to attempt such a task, even if they had shovels and tools. The avalanche had smashed everything in its path. A search yielded one shattered tent pole. That was all.

Some men might have flown into a panic, Jerry thought, but Dr. Sebold never lost his calm. "Our situation could be worse," he told the group. "We're going to be almighty hungry and cold and tired before it gets better. But we can thank the good Lord we weren't buried in our sleep."

"It's a long way back to base camp, Carl."

"Four days, I figure. And every day a misery. But we can't stay here."

Emptying their pockets they pooled what food they had: four candy bars, three packets of soup concentrate and a box of raisins. Less than two pounds to feed eleven men for at least four days. Twelve hours since their last meal. Already Jerry felt ravenous.

"How? Down the gorge again?"

"That's right," Dr. Sebold said grimly. "If a starving ten-year-old boy can do it, so can we."

Four nights later the exhausted members of Team One staggered across the meadow into base camp. To Jerry his own home had never looked more welcome than the familiar sight of tents in Terang Valley. The last thing he remembered before flopping into bed was Dr. Baimbridge tugging off his boots. He slept for fourteen solid hours.

Afterwards the Balu Kosi trip seemed dreamlike and unreal, a kind of nightmare. But parts of that experience stood out bold and clear, never to be forgotten. He had chased a yeti, or something, up a mountain. He had lived through an avalanche. He had learned how it was to go without food, and how men shared hardship. They had failed in their mission, but they had helped to save two human lives.

Dr. Baimbridge told of his struggle to bring the Tibetans out to safety several days before. After a rest he had sent them on to the head village of the district, where they would stay with other refugees.

"The boy—I never did learn his name—left this for you." The doctor handed Jerry a slab of driftwood. "He made it himself."

The words *Om mane padme om,* the sacred Tibetan prayer, had been laboriously carved out with a knife.

"He said if you hadn't found him and his grandfather they would have died. He's going to pray for you every day."

Malloy's team had not returned yet. There was still hope they might have been successful. But the doctor vetoed Jerry's suggestion that Team One fill the time by making another reconnaissance climb.

"Young bucks like you and Rick bounce back in a hurry. But us oldsters, Carl and Lars and myself, need more time to recuperate. We're all taking it easy the next few days."

That was so, Jerry realized. He and Rick, after a few extra meals, felt as fit as ever. But the older men showed lingering effects of their ordeal on the Balu Kosi. Dr. Sebold had lost pounds and Johansen's feet were a mass of sores.

"I have another patient," the doctor said. "Big Red. Frankly I'm worried about him."

They walked to the cage. The bear lunged up, growling, and made a vicious swipe at the bars. Then he slumped back and lay glaring at them with glazed eyes, breathing hoarsely. When Jerry ventured a step closer, Big Red snapped at his outstretched arm.

"He's never acted like that since we caught him."

"He won't eat. Roars at everybody who comes near."

"Maybe somebody gave him poisoned meat," Rick said.

He called over the three Nepalis who had been left behind on guard duty. They assured him they had fed and watered the bear faithfully. No stranger had been in camp during the expedition's absence. About a week ago, they said, Big Red had begun to behave strangely, as though he were sick.

"I'm no vet," Dr. Baimbridge said, "but I think he has an infection. And if it doesn't clear up soon, we might lose him."

"Can't we give him a hypo so you can examine him?"

"He'd tear off your arm if you got within reach. Without that knockout gun our hands are tied."

Twice Jerry tried to edge up to the cage but each time Big Red, although visibly weaker, growled and bared his fangs. There was no safe approach, no way they could rope or subdue him. By the following day he was too feeble to stand on his legs. They could only stand by helplessly and watch. *We can't let him die,* Jerry told himself. *Somehow we have to save him.*

"There's one thing we might try," Rick said.

"What?"

"The more I think about Tom Malloy's rifle the more convinced I am that it's somewhere near camp. If we can find it."

"But if one of the men from the village stole it—"

"We haven't proved that yet. Are you willing to gamble a few hours' time?"

Jerry nodded. Anything was better than this.

"Use your imagination now. Pretend you're the thief. You've just sneaked out of Malloy's tent. It's dark but people are milling around. Any minute, any second, you may be discovered. You do the first thing that pops into your head. So where would you hide anything the size of that rifle?"

"Dig a hole and bury it?"

"You don't have time. Besides the fresh dirt would give it away."

Jerry peered off across the meadow toward the trees. *Not there*, he decided. *Too far from camp. Not in the grass, nor in the rocks. Too easy to find.* Then he snapped his fingers. "Sure, I'd chuck it in the creek."

Rick slapped him on the back. "Elementary, my dear Watson. So obvious we never thought of it. Come on!"

Although the idea seemed far-fetched to Jerry, they got two long poles and climbed down the bank. Unlike mountain streams he knew back home, this was an opaque chalky gray, fed by glaciers. There were no clear, sparkling pools with gravel bottoms and lurking trout. Each pool had to be probed. Working opposite sides of the creek, they poked under boulders and pried up rocks. It was slow, strenuous work. By the end of two hours they had covered less than fifty yards.

He was glad they had no audience. This snipe hunt seemed crazier by the minute. "Current could have carried it clear down to the river," he grumbled. "If it ever was here."

But Rick refused to give up. "Let's try downstream."

The pools were larger and deeper here, and the water swifter. Gritting his teeth, Jerry waded out above his knees and went on jabbing with his pole. Something turned under the pressure and fell back into a still deeper pothole before he could grab it. It felt like the right size and weight, but then again it could have been a water-logged branch.

He was sopping wet and mad now, stubborn mad. He peeled off his shirt and submerged, groping blindly for the bottom. His fingers brushed wood and slipped off, and he had to surface, sputtering for breath. On his second dive he got a firm grip on something, gave a tug and came up with it in both hands. He shook the water out of his eyes and stared.

It was the missing rifle.

Rick let out a whoop. "Jackpot!"

He waded back to the bank, wiped off the mud, and peered down the barrel. "Not too badly rusted," he said and passed the rifle to Rick. "It took a beating on those rocks, but some gun oil and elbow grease ought to fix it up."

"How long do you suppose it's been here?"

"Since the night we caught Big Red."

"No villager would have thrown this rifle in a creek. I'll tell you when it happened, Jerry. The night you tripped Malloy's burglar alarm. Think back."

He tried to think back, to recall the details. The whole camp, aroused by the noise, had rushed to the supply tent. But he only assumed that. He didn't know for certain. It would have been a perfect opportunity for someone to loot Malloy's tent while attention was diverted elsewhere.

"We've been barking up the wrong tree," Rick went on. "This narrows it down."

"How do you mean?"

"The thief is somebody in this camp. Not an outsider." Rick grinned. "I'd like to see his face when he learns we've found it."

"Any ideas?"

"Maybe. You go look after your bear. I'm going to prowl around some more."

Jerry carried the rifle back to the tent, stripped it down, and cleaned and oiled the parts. Until today he had been skeptical of Rick's suspicions. He still was. They had no proof that the culprit was one of their own men. He hated to believe that. He could not imagine the motive, beyond sheer vandalism, that had prompted such a senseless act. But no other reasonable explanation occurred to him.

Dr. Sebold and the other men were equally puzzled when he told them the story. If they suspected anyone they kept it to themselves. The consensus was that the thief had been frightened off and never dared return to fish the rifle out of the creek.

"I know this much," Dr. Sebold said. "Tom Malloy will be pleased. And we can take those guards off now. This isn't likely to happen again."

"Malloy won't be any more pleased than I am," Dr. Baimbridge said, "if that blunderbuss of his still works. Come along, young fellow."

Jerry mixed up a batch of the drug solution, filled a syringe and charged the rifle with CO_2. Standing well back from the cage, he fired a dart into Big Red's shoulder. Two minutes later the bear collapsed.

They hauled his inert hulk out onto the grass. The doctor rolled up his sleeves and knelt down gingerly. With a stick he propped open the bear's mouth, then flashed a tiny light down his throat, into his nostrils and ears. "Ha!" he muttered. "Abscess. Thought so."

He lanced the infected ear, injected a hypodermic of penicillin, and smeared on salve. Through all this Big Red's eyes remained open. He could see and smell and hear, Dr. Baimbridge explained, but his motor nerves were immobilized. When the doctor finally stood up a broad smile crossed his dripping face. "Some sawbones, eh?" he said and winked at Jerry. "But next time I wish you'd trim the patient's toenails. They make me nervous."

"How is he, doctor?"

"This should bring down the fever. We'll give him another shot later. Our hairy friend's going to feel like a pincushion before he gets well."

They gave Big Red a second treatment that afternoon, and a third the following morning. By then he showed definite improvement. He ate and paced up and down with something like his old spirit. Jerry covered his cage at night against the drafts, brought fresh grass for him to roll on and special tidbits to eat. No bedridden invalid could have received better care. Within another twenty-four hours the doctor pronounced him out of danger.

That same night Malloy's team returned from Khumbu Glacier. Jerry was shocked by their appearance. They looked drawn and gray and bone-tired. Malloy, with Howe and Conrad and their bearers, had traveled some three hundred miles in three weeks. They had crossed two high passes and climbed one peak, all without success. Through Ang Nuri they had questioned every Sherpa they met along the way. Nobody had seen or heard of yeti tracks anywhere in the entire region.

"These people have a dozen different explanations to account for it," Malloy said. "They claim the weather's too hot this year for yetis, or too cold, or too wet, or too dry. They say all these expeditions lately have driven the yetis away. Some believe they've been exterminated by a strange disease. Take your pick."

"There is another belief," Rick said. "The curse."

"I never heard of that one."

"Anyone who looks upon a yeti bears a curse. That's why the Sherpas tell you these wild tales. They mean well."

"It's like chasing ghosts," Malloy said bitterly.

"Ghosts don't leave footprints in the snow. Or cry in the night. All we can do is keep on looking, Tom. And hope."

"But we have so little time left. Barely a month."

"Cheer up," Dr. Sebold said. "Anyway we got your rifle back. Jerry found it in the creek."

"In the creek?" Malloy stared at him and said sharply, "What made you look there?"

Jerry flushed and glanced at Rick. If he told why, Rick would be on a spot, trying to explain all his vague suspicions. This was not the time. He said lamely, "Well, it seemed the last place left that we hadn't searched."

"Funny you're the only one who thought of it, Dunham."

"You can argue about that tomorrow," Dr. Baimbridge broke in. "Right now you and Ross and John are turning in. You look like the devil. Doctor's orders." Fussing like a mother hen, he shooed them off to bed.

Later, in the privacy of their own tent, Rick said indignantly, "How do you like that? Malloy didn't even say 'thanks.'"

"You know what I think," Jerry said. "He has a sneaky hunch I threw his rifle in the creek myself. Just to spite him."

"I have a better hunch." Rick lowered his voice to a whisper. "Malloy wasn't surprised tonight or pleased. He was mad."

"So?"

"Malloy stole his own rifle. Don't ask me why. I don't know yet. But when I do—" Rick burrowed down in his cot and refused to answer any more questions.

Most of the camp was still asleep when Jerry got up to feed Big Red early next morning. Glancing up, he saw two men running down the trail from Terang. One was the *shikar*, the other a stranger. "Yeti!" the *shikar* shouted at the top of his lungs and waved his arms. "Yeti!"

Jerry poked his head back into the tent. "Rick, come out here, will you. Something about yetis, but that's the only word I understand."

Tousled and sleepy-eyed, Rick stumbled outside in his pajamas, whereupon the *shikar* burst into an excited monologue. Slowly a broad smile spread across Rick's face. "They've come to claim the reward."

"What reward?"

"The hundred rupees we offered." Rick indicated the stranger. "He's found yeti tracks. Fresh ones!"

CHAPTER 12

IS name was Tarke, a woodcutter of Terang. He had
been returning from a visit to another village five days
distant, so he told Rick, and decided to take a route
unfamiliar to him which was said to be shorter. He had missed
the trail and spent the night in a valley high up on a peak
known as Kang. During the night he had heard a sound as
though someone were throwing rocks. Thoroughly frightened,
he left the place as soon as it was light enough to travel safely,
and so had come upon the tracks of a single yeti nearby.

There was no question the tracks were new. They had not
been there the night before. Tarke was convinced the yeti
had been throwing rocks at him, to drive him away.

Would he be willing to guide the expedition *sahibs* back to

136

this valley, for an additional one hundred rupees? Tarke shook his head emphatically. No, he would not return. He had received his warning, and like any sensible man, knew when he was well off. No offer of money or gifts would change his mind.

Everybody in camp had gathered to hear his story, and a number of villagers had followed also, forming a considerable crowd. "He's really afraid," Rick explained, acting as interpreter. "Remember that curse I told you about last night? Well, Tarke believes in it. He's so afraid that he's going to pay good money to hire a *bon-po*."

"What's a *bon-po?*"

"Sherpa witch doctor. If the yeti has put some bad demons in his brain, the *bon-po* will try to cast them out."

"Do you believe he actually saw footprints?" Malloy asked. "Or did he invent this story to collect the reward?"

After another lengthy exchange, Rick said, "According to Tarke this valley is easy to locate. He'll show us on the map. If we go there and don't find any tracks, then we don't owe him a cent."

"That's a fair offer." Dr. Sebold brought out his map case, and for several minutes he, Rick, and Tarke engaged in a bilingual, three-way discussion, which ended with Tarke sketching his own map and landmarks on a separate sheet of paper. "There's only one thing I don't like about his story," Dr. Sebold said. "The location. Kang Peak is right on the Tibetan frontier. Ask him if he ran into any patrols, Rick."

Tarke had not. He was, he admitted, more afraid of yetis than of Chinese soldiers.

Dr. Baimbridge wanted to know the approximate elevation. Tarke, who did not measure either in English feet or European meters, could tell him only that it was very high and cold. This was the sum total of his information.

"Those tracks will be at least a week old before we can get there," Dr. Sebold said. "But it's our only lead."

"I don't think we should gamble that much time on the word of a man who may be lying," Malloy said.

"Rick believes him, Tom. So does the *shikar*. They were right before."

"So it's Kang Peak then?"

"Unless anybody has a better suggestion."

Nobody did.

"Let's see. If we leave tomorrow—"

But Dr. Baimbridge put his foot down. "Nobody leaves this camp tomorrow, Carl. Nor the next day. Even then I'm not sure all of us will be in shape to go. The human body can take just so much punishment."

They argued, but Dr. Baimbridge held firm. He was responsible for the health of every expedition member. Both teams, he pointed out, had been through a grueling time at high altitudes. It was dangerous for them to climb again without sufficient rest. Reluctantly Dr. Sebold gave in, and agreed to a departure date three days later.

This, everyone knew now, would be their last major effort. The elements of time and weather were closing in. That night's radio broadcast brought the news that a storm front, long overdue, was forming far to the south in the Indian Ocean. It might break up. But if it continued to grow and moved northward across India into Nepal too quickly, they might not be able to reach the Kang region at all.

The announcer also told of further anti-American demonstrations in Katmandu. A student had been arrested for painting the words YANKEE GO HOME on the walls of an American mission.

"Communists," Rick muttered. "Stirring up more trouble."

Jerry switched off the set. Whenever he looked at the prayer board which the Tibetan boy had made for him, the subject of Communists seemed all too real and close.

He crossed to Big Red's cage and covered it for the night. The bear lay quietly and did not growl. He was completely well, the doctor had said that afternoon, when they had taken him out for a final examination. Well and ready for the long trip ahead. Jerry grinned at him through the bars. "The Yanks are going home pretty soon, Red," he said. "But you're going with us."

He got up earlier than usual next morning. There was an English-language news broadcast at that hour and he was anxious to have the latest report on the storm front. But reception was so poor he could make out only a few words. Leaving the radio, he walked to the mess tent and opened the meat cache he had lashed to a pole above the ground, to keep it beyond reach of any stray dogs.

This was Big Red's supply and he was surprised to find it empty except for one small deer haunch. He made a mental note to ask the village hunters to bring in a fresh supply, and went on to the cage. Even before he folded back the tarp cover he sensed something wrong. The wooden peg that held the door dangled from its leather thong, and the door itself creaked on its hinges as it swung slightly back and forth in the wind.

Incredulous, he stared into the empty cage. Big Red was gone.

In a state of shock he looked back at camp, half-expecting to see the bear lumber out from behind a tent. How? his mind asked dully. How could it happen? How could the bear have gotten out?

Then he recovered quickly. Never mind how, he thought. Get him back first. Questions later.

Huge pawprints, plain in the wet grass, led down to the creek and disappeared among the rocks. Big Red had taken to the water. Jerry had to remind himself that Big Red was no tame mascot, although at times he had seemed like one. He was a creature of the wild, and back to the wild he had gone, as fast as he could travel. To recapture him would be more than a one-man job.

Within ten minutes Dr. Sebold, wakened by his shout, had mobilized every man in camp to join the search. Malloy loaded up his rifle; Rick raced to the village for reinforcements. Dorje, Tandu, Ang, and the other Sherpas and Nepalis scattered along the creek to look for signs. Then John Conrad found fresh droppings and the hunt swung upstream.

Shortly Rick returned with the *shikar* and several hunters, accompanied by their mastiffs. Yapping and baying in a frenzy of excitement, the dogs picked up the scent and scrambled over the glacial moraine, while the men fell far behind. Hope grew faint as they climbed on and on. It was evident now that Big Red, in his bid for freedom, would run himself to death rather than be retaken.

By midday they had trailed him to the foot of the glacier. The *shikar* put his dogs on leash and conferred with Rick. With such a long headstart, he said, the great red *balu* had escaped into the ice. Oh, he was a cunning one! He knew the ice would dull the scent sense of any dog. He would hide himself on the glacier, living off his fat until hunger drove him out once more. Then it might be possible to catch him, but today the gods had not smiled upon the *sahibs*.

The *shikar* spread his palms upward in a sign of regret. He had done his best. If the *sahibs* insisted, he would go on with the hunt, but—

Jerry peered at the blue-green masses of ice. To make an assault on the glacier they would need to pack up the necessary equipment. Even then it might take days to run Big Red to earth. Big Red, he knew, was gone for good.

Sunk in gloom, he followed the others wearily back to camp. Now that he had time to ponder the question, he felt sure that someone, the same someone who had stolen Malloy's rifle, must have tampered with Big Red's cage. Big Red hadn't scratched or smashed his way out. There were no tooth- or clawmarks on the door and the bars were intact.

"You and Baimbridge had the bear out of the cage yesterday afternoon," Dr. Sebold said. "Was that the last time you opened the door?"

"No, I opened it once more. To put in fresh grass."

"And closed it up tight afterward, I suppose?"

Jerry nodded. "I pounded the peg down through the hasp

like I always do. He couldn't have pushed it open himself."

"Are you sure you did?" Malloy said.

"Positive."

"Well, of course if you're sure—" Malloy's shrug implied that he, for one, was not. "Or else that bear was a wizard at picking locks."

"Somebody deliberately loosened the peg, Dr. Malloy, and let him escape."

"And who would this mysterious Mr. X be?" Malloy asked.

"I don't know who. I don't know why. But that's how it happened," Jerry said stubbornly.

It would have been simple. Three days ago Dr. Sebold had pulled off the guards. Then last night someone, Malloy's Mr. X, had taken meat from the cache, tossed it in front of the cage and unfastened the door. Big Red, sniffing food, had done the rest. The trouble was, he couldn't prove it. Tom Malloy, and possibly others, suspected that his carelessness had cost the expedition a prize specimen.

There had been the yeti skin first. Then the truck smashup. The rifle. And now Big Red. Whatever he might say would sound like another alibi, like the boy who called "Wolf!" once too often. *Dunham's done it again*, Malloy would say in his sarcastic way; *the original mess-off kid*.

"Let's forget it," Dr. Sebold said curtly. "It's water under the bridge now. We're leaving for Kang Peak in two days. We'll concentrate on that."

For once Jerry found he took no pleasure in getting ready for the next hunt. He wanted to be alone, to think this out.

Somewhere there had to be an answer to the string of bad breaks that had dogged the expedition from its start. The weather, an avalanche, an emergency appendectomy, all these were acts of Nature, and therefore could be ruled out. The others had been man-made. Made or caused by one of twenty-four men, excluding Rick and himself. A man in this camp.

He could not duck the issue any longer. Big Red's escape had been one coincidence too many. Back in his tent he wrote out a list of names, trying to find some pattern or common denominator that would link one individual to the "accidents." In every case he had been involved to some degree. But why? Why? He asked himself again and again, and came up with no logical solution.

It was almost dark when he quit. He glanced at his watch and turned on the radio for the weather broadcast, wondering how the storm front had developed. Waiting for the tubes to warm up, he reached for his notepad and then frowned. There was no receiver hum, no glow on the panel light. He checked the battery connections and peered into the back of the set. Abruptly his body stiffened.

After a stunned moment he got up and stepped outside. Several of the men stood chatting by the mess tent and he walked toward them, trying to appear casual. Presently Dr. Sebold noticed him and said, "How's the forecast tonight, Jerry?"

"Could I see you for a minute?"

Dr. Sebold broke away from the group and followed him back to the tent. Jerry snapped on his flashlight and directed the beam into the radio case, revealing a snarl of broken glass and tangled wire. Somebody had smashed the tubes and relays with a hammer, or possibly a rock.

Dr. Sebold whistled softly. "When did you discover this?"

"Just now. From the outside it looks all right. It worked this morning."

"Can you repair it?"

"Not with the spare parts we have. Anyway, it would take an expert, and I'm not that."

The director's face was solemn as he looked up at Jerry. Jerry swallowed. He had been in his tent most of the afternoon. So the radio had been wrecked some time that morning, when everybody was off chasing Big Red. Somebody, Mr. X again, could have doubled back to camp, done his work and overtaken the stragglers later. That seemed to be his method, to create a diversion and then strike.

"Dr. Sebold, you don't believe I had anything to do with this?"

"Jerry—" The director put a hand on his shoulder. "For a long time I've known something was wrong. I'm not as blind as Rick Dawa thinks. I want to give my men every benefit of the doubt. I won't accuse anybody without proof. Perhaps I've been too easygoing. But you're the last one I'd suspect."

"Thank you, sir."

"The fact is, we have a saboteur on our hands, Jerry. I don't know what his game is. But if we give him enough rope he's bound to hang himself before long."

"Something like Malloy's burglar alarm?"

"It has to be cleverer than that."

Jerry thought for a minute. "Maybe if we fake the weather reports, pretend that I've fixed the radio. That might fool him."

"It's worth a try. And I have a wrinkle or two of my own. But Jerry—" Dr. Sebold's grip tightened. "Whatever you do, be careful. This fellow is slippery and maybe dangerous. And he must be desperate to take such chances."

"What about the storm front? Now that we've lost contact we can't tell if it's moving in or not."

Dr. Sebold smiled faintly. "We're going to tackle Kang Peak, storm or no storm. That's how desperate I am."

Next morning Jerry got the spare-parts kit from the supply tent and sat outside tinkering with the radio. It was strictly window dressing. A repair job this complex was far beyond his limited experience. But Mr. X might not be aware of that. He went on with his act, sure that word would spread through camp.

Some while later he noticed a native approaching by the lower trail. The stranger, a Nepali, set down his heavy pack among the tents and spoke briefly to Rick. Then the shout went up, "Mail! Come and get it! Mail!"

Everyone ran. They had received no mail for months, nor expected any until they returned to Katmandu. His father, Rick explained, had hired a runner to bring this load up from the city, knowing how starved they must be for news from home. This was Mr. Dawa's treat for the expedition.

And treat it was, a real bonanza. Sprawled out on the grass, Jerry greedily devoured every letter. There were several from his parents, one from Mr. Trevor, from his roommate at State and other friends. There was a copy of the hometown newspaper with his picture on the front page. His mother had sent a box of cookies, now stale and crumbled. Even so, they tasted wonderful.

Rick's father, they all agreed, deserved a medal. They laughed and read bits of news aloud to one another. For a while the mood of gloom and suspicion which had gripped the camp was dispelled.

Then Rick caught Jerry's eyes and the old feeling crept right back. Rick was on the bloodhound trail again.

Later, when they were alone, Rick handed him a letter. "Here's what I've been waiting for. This old family friend is head of the Zoology Department at Eastern University, actually Tom Malloy's boss. Before we left Katmandu I wrote and asked him, in confidence, for a report on Malloy. Go ahead, read his answer."

Jerry scanned the typewritten pages. Malloy was a brilliant mammalogist, the letter said, perhaps a bit erratic and ambitious, but nevertheless one of the best in his field. He had counted on being named director of the Trevor Himalayan Expedition, since he had taken part in two previous expeditions to the same region, and considered himself uniquely qualified. The appointment of Carl Sebold in his place had come as a bitter shock. He had regarded this as a blow to his career. Only with the greatest effort had he been persuaded to go as second in command.

"For a long time," Rick said, "I thought our troubles were some kind of a Communist plot. But this letter clears up everything."

"Does it?"

"The man's sick with envy. He has to be top dog, or else. You notice how he tears down every suggestion Dr. Sebold makes, argues and raises objections. He's out to wreck this expedition. He'll make sure we never find a yeti."

"That's like cutting off your nose to spite your face," Jerry said.

"Not the way he thinks. When he gets back to America he can say: 'I told you so. None of this would have happened if I'd been director. Next time give me the job.'"

"But—"

"Wait. Here's Malloy's record. One," Rick held up a finger, "he was the last person to drive that truck. Two, he just happens to be taking a walk the night a prowler comes to camp. Three, he installs a burglar trap and then forgets it. Four, somebody steals his rifle from under his cot. Five, the night he gets back from Khumbu the bear escapes. We can't pin the radio on him yet, but he knows how much we need those weather reports."

"Sounds pretty black when you put it that way."

"He always blames somebody else, mostly you. But now that we know his motive it all adds up."

"It still adds up to a lot of suspicion. That letter isn't proof."

"Don't you believe it?"

"Tom Malloy is bitter and hard to live with. He seems to have a grudge against the world. I feel sorry for him. But I think he's too good a scientist to sabotage our work like that."

"What if you're wrong? No telling what he might do next."

"Do me a favor, will you, Rick. Keep this letter under your hat for now. Till we get back from Kang Peak. I have an idea how we'll catch our man."

"All right," Rick agreed. "I guess it's your turn to play detective."

CHAPTER 13

PERATION Kang, as they came to call the last hunt, got under way on a cold, drizzly morning. Only five of the staff assembled with their packs in the wet gray dawn. Neither Johansen nor Dr. Baimbridge had entirely recovered from the Balu Kosi trip, and Ross Howe decided he should stay behind to make recordings of the native music. So far he had been forced to neglect his anthropological studies for the expedition.

Dr. Sebold looked drawn and ill. "You shouldn't be going either, Carl," the doctor advised him. "Your body is not a machine."

He grinned. "Nothing like a little exercise to tone up the system. Take care of my boys, Harold."

A number of the bearers, suffering from various complaints, also had to be left behind. It was a small group that filed across the meadow. Jerry glanced back at Big Red's empty cage, at the row of tents, and then a curtain of rain cut them from view.

For two days they traveled to the north and east under leaden skies. The weather alternated between rain squalls and blinding flurries of sleet. Fording one swollen stream after another, they climbed above timber line, above all vegetation, into a barren world of rock. That night they camped at sixteen thousand four hundred feet. The temperature dropped to ten degrees and a frigid wind buffeted their tents. They could not judge whether this was merely a local disturbance or the prelude to a major storm.

In the morning Dr. Sebold was barely able to crawl out of his sleeping bag. He drank some tea, took one of the pills the doctor had prescribed, and struggled into his clothes. His face was gray and blotchy and his teeth chattered. "Be all right in a bit," he mumbled. "You fellows go on. I'll catch up."

Malloy exchanged a look with the others. By now they all could recognize the symptoms of altitude sickness: fatigue, chills, and slurred speech, the result of prolonged physical and mental strain. "Carl," he said, "you can't go any farther."

"Have to go on. Have to—"

"Listen to me, Carl. You're sick, worn out. You have to rest."

Protesting weakly, Dr. Sebold lay back while Malloy discussed this newest crisis with John Conrad, Rick, and Jerry. It was vital to get the director down to a lower elevation at once, which left two alternatives. Either they could call off the hunt and all return to base camp, or split forces and send him back with an escort.

"We can't gamble on the weather," Conrad pointed out. "That storm front may be right behind us."

"Carl himself wants us to go on," Malloy said. "It's probably our last chance. I'll take the responsibility."

And so it was decided. Dorje and Gylgen, the two strongest Sherpas, would take Dr. Sebold back to Terang by slow, easy stages. The others would push ahead to Kang Peak. Tents and food supplies were divided. They shook hands and said goodbye, not very cheerfully. "You're in charge now, Tom," Dr. Sebold said. "It's up to you. Just remember, leave yourself a safety margin in case anything goes wrong."

As they turned up the trail, Jerry thought of the letter Rick had received from his zoologist friend. Tom Malloy had been granted his wish at last. He was temporary leader of the expedition.

The day brought little relief from the bitter cold but late that afternoon, after they had climbed nearly fifteen hundred feet, the skies cleared briefly. The summit of the peak stood out and by consulting the woodcutter's sketch they knew they were near the valley where he had seen yeti tracks. Some nine days had passed. The yeti might be miles away. But the prospect of tomorrow's search buoyed up their spirits as they pitched camp.

After midnight the storm struck with whiplash fury. It began as a low moaning of the wind. Guy ropes hummed with the vibration and tugged at their stakes. There was a lull and then the wind rose to a shriek, battering the walls and snapping the nylon flaps like pistol shots. It beat against their eardrums, a deafening maniac din they could not escape. They could only burrow deeper into their bags and pray the tents would hold.

After daybreak the snow began, first as feathery flakes and then as wind-driven pellets that stung the face like buckshot. By noon the tents were half-buried and sagging dangerously under the weight. They dug out, and dug out again, and the snow piled steadily higher, until their camp resembled a tiny pit encircled by a white stockade. Cramped three men to a tent, they could barely turn over to eat and sleep. Tempers frayed and quarrels flared over trifles. Not even Rick's unfailing humor could boost morale. They were captives of the storm.

Then, after three days, it blew out with a final dying whimper. They crawled out and gazed about at the silent landscape. Deep snow covered the rocks in every direction. "We've had it this time," Conrad said. "Might as well pack up and head down."

"We've come this far," Malloy said. "Let's look around first."

"In that new snow? It's up to our necks."

But in the end Malloy had his way. They agreed to wait one more day for the snow crust to harden. Then they would split into two three-man teams, climb to the valley, search as far as they could in a single day, and return to advance camp.

"One day, Tom," Conrad insisted. "That's all. If we don't find anything by then, I'm pulling out."

Early next morning they separated, Malloy and Jerry and Ang in Team One; Conrad and Tandu and Rick in Team Two. Malloy carried the rifle, Jerry the walkie-talkie. In their light packs each man carried emergency rations in case, for any reason, they should not get back before dark.

The valley proved to be a shallow bowl several miles long and broken by many low ridges. Radio communication, Jerry saw, was going to be difficult, if not impossible. By keeping to the crests, where snow was seldom knee-deep, they made fairly good time, and by midday reached the base of Kang Peak itself. The sky was clear, the sun warm, and they halted for a bite to eat.

Malloy got out the sketch again and studied it. "This should be the spot," he said. "But I still think that woodcutter made it up."

Jerry glanced at his watch. "We'll have to start back before too long."

And then they saw the tracks. They stretched across the snow from south to north in a single line, fresh and clear and evenly spaced. A yeti, a large one, had passed this way since the storm, possibly that morning.

"By thunder!" Malloy's eyes danced with excitement. "We're right on his heels!"

He filled a syringe and loaded the rifle, while Jerry tried without success to raise Team Two. "Yeti go very fast, *sahib*," Ang spoke up. "No catch 'em today, I think."

"We'll never have a better chance. Come on. Hurry, man!"

At a fast walk they set out on the trail. It led along the ridge summit, following each dip and rise, then climbed to a bald, rocky point where the wind had scoured away all snow. Here the tracks vanished but Malloy circled back and forth until he picked up the trail on the far side and they pushed ahead almost at a trot.

The valley lay behind them now and they began descending a long rough slope. An hour went by, then two, and the shadow of Kang Peak lengthened across the snow. Jerry's eyes ached from the strain of peering ahead for a glimpse of a dark figure, but there was only the dazzling glare, a wilderness of white. Sweat poured down his face. His side hurt. But he would have dropped in exhaustion before asking Tom Malloy to stop and rest.

It was Ang Nuri who stopped first. The Sherpa turned a gray face to the sky and said, "No go farther."

Malloy snorted. "Why not?"

"Border that way." Ang swung an arm to the north. "Too close now."

"Border? You don't think I'm going to let a line on some map stop me."

"Plenty bad, *sahib*. Is much danger. Ang Nuri know."

"What's wrong with you, Ang? There isn't a Red within fifty miles."

But Ang shook his head. No appeal or argument would sway him. He was genuinely frightened. And Jerry, remembering the Tibetan boy and the slaughtered yak, could not blame him. "*Sahib* go on, Ang go back," he repeated stubbornly.

Malloy turned to Jerry in disgust. "How about you, Dunham? Getting cold feet too?"

Jerry hesitated. "I'll go with you," he said.

They left Ang and followed the trail down the next draw, presently emerging on a boulder-strewn plain. Malloy set a furious pace and Jerry, determined not to fall behind, plowed along in his tracks. The yeti apparently had a definite destination in mind. His footprints led on and on, straight into the north.

Blue shadows lay over the land and the inevitable wind sprang up. It was late. Jerry felt the weariness creep up his legs. Rick and Conrad would be back at the tents, wondering about them. Even if they turned back now, they would never reach camp before dark. They would have to spend part of the night in the open, without shelter or fuel for a fire. He should have gone back with Ang. He should go back now. To blazes with Tom Malloy, yeti or no yeti.

The trail made an abrupt right-angle turn. The footprints, now farther apart, lead into a field of boulders. "Broke into a run," Malloy observed. "Something must have scared him."

"Maybe he saw us."

Malloy unslung the rifle from his back and started on. But a line of dots on a rise off to their right caught Jerry's attention. "You coming?" Malloy called impatiently.

Jerry pointed. "Over there."

Malloy turned, stared. A curious change came over his face. "Looks like more tracks."

Together they hurried up the rise. Suddenly Jerry felt the

hair rise on the nape of his neck. The "dots" he had seen were footprints. Not animal tracks. Human bootprints.

He peered up at the top of the slope. Several men had come down partway, stopped, and turned back. The yeti had sighted or scented them, and bounded off in alarm. That much was clear. But where were they now? And *who* were they?

"You don't suppose—" Malloy began. Before he could finish his sentence four soldiers sprang up from behind the rocks on either side.

They wore gray uniforms, heavily padded against the cold, and billed caps with the five-starred insignia of Red China, and three of them carried rifles. All were young, but they looked grim and efficient and ready to shoot if necessary. The fourth, who brandished a pistol, seemed to be some kind of officer. He barked a command. Malloy raised his arms and Jerry followed suit.

The officer, obviously puzzled, fired questions at them in Chinese, to all of which they could only shake their heads. At length he gave up, then confiscated Malloy's rifle and the walkie-talkie and their two packs. They were roughly searched and at rifle point herded into line behind the officer. With the other three Chinese prodding them from behind, they set out once more to the north.

"Where do you think they're taking us?" Jerry asked.

A soldier bawled at him, and Malloy said, "Better not talk now. Watch me and do what I do."

They tramped on in silence as the twilight thickened. Jerry was too stunned to feel immediate fear. That would come later. They must have crossed the frontier into Tibet, he thought, possibly before he and Malloy had blundered onto the patrol. The soldiers had seen them coming and hidden among the rocks. If they had listened to Ang Nuri's advice, if they had turned back sooner—if.

But they had rushed on blindly, following the yeti. It was too late for regrets and might-have-been's. They were prisoners. Every step took them farther from help, deeper into Communist territory.

The plateau across which they had been traveling looked flat, but just before dark they came to a narrow defile. Climbing down the trail, they saw at the bottom a small, windowless stone house half-covered with drift snow. The officer threw back the animal hide that served as a door and waved them in. One of the soldiers lighted a tallow dip while another built a fire of twigs and yak dung and pumped it into a bright yellow flame with a hand bellows.

Thankful to be out of the wind and cold, Jerry peered about the hut's interior. It was cone-shaped, like a beehive, with a hole at the top for smoke, and had a sour smell of sweat and grease and damp wool. Debris littered the earthen floor and there was no furniture, only a pile of dirty blankets, an ammunition box, and a few cooking utensils. He and Malloy were motioned into a corner where they sat under the officer's watchful eye.

The others boiled up a mess of rice and presently began to eat, picking their portions out of the pot with chopsticks and gulping down bowls of tea. Jerry tried not to think of food. It was hours since he had eaten, and then only a snack. But the Chinese made no offer to share their rations.

The officer, who had been examining Malloy's rifle, grunted with excitement. There followed a heated exchange among the four Chinese, but the officer silenced all argument by snapping an order. Two of the soldiers grumbled and put on their coats and gathered their rifles. The hide door flapped shut behind them as they stepped out and an icy draft crept across the floor. The remaining soldier brought the officer some tea and squatted down beside the fire.

"Jerry." Malloy's gruff voice startled him in the stillness. "You're a good kid. I'm sorry I've given you such a rough time."

The officer looked up sharply and frowned, but made no threatening move.

"He doesn't understand English," Malloy went on. "He thinks we're American spies."

"Spies? How do you know?"

"I was a prisoner in Korea during the war. I picked up a little Mandarin. But I don't want him to know that."

"What's he going to do with us?"

"He's not sure what to do. That's why he sent those two soldiers off, to get orders from his superior. This is just an outpost, but there's a frontier garrison not far from here."

"They won't turn us loose, will they? Not if they think we're spies."

"I'm afraid not. We're a big catch to the Chinese. More important than any yeti. They'll probably march us into the interior for questioning."

The officer lighted a cigarette and gazed at them thoughtfully through the smoke, as though trying to make sense out of their talk. The soldier, rifle across his knees, stared at them with dull eyes.

"There's only two now," Jerry said. "Maybe we could rush them."

"Not a chance. These monkeys mean business. They'd shoot us before we got started."

Jerry glanced at the big red-haired scientist. He had never thought of Tom Malloy as a soldier and prisoner of war. This was another side to this strange man, who could speak so calmly of being shot. Even now he found it hard to dislike him.

"I got us into this mess," Malloy went on. "Me and my bull-headedness. I deserve whatever's coming. But you don't, Jerry. I'll get you out if I can."

"I'm not blaming you. I didn't have to come along."

"Wait till you hear the rest. I want to get this off my chest. Remember the yeti skin?"

Jerry nodded.

"It's not lost. It's safe in New York City. I got a letter in that batch of mail the other day. While we were staying at that hotel, apparently I packed the skin with some other stuff by mistake, and left it with my brother. He found it and wrote me, but no mail caught up with us for months."

"But why—"

"Why didn't I admit my mistake and face the music? Because I'd acted like such a darn fool. Ashamed, I guess."

Jerry stirred uncomfortably and the officer, instantly alert, shifted the pistol in his lap. The soldier tossed another chunk of fuel on the fire and dipped more tea from the pot. A gust of wind rattled the hide over the doorway.

And then Jerry, in spite of everything, felt a warmth flowing back into him. Malloy's admission had cleared the air between them. Malloy was an ally, not an enemy. They were on the same team. "I have a confession too," he said. "For a long while I half-believed you were a Red agent, out to wreck the expedition."

"Me?" Malloy grinned wryly. "I spent two years in Red prison camps. Another year in Army hospitals recovering. Three years. I guess that's why I drove myself so hard, and everybody else. Trying to make up for lost time."

Then his eyes sobered again. "We don't have much time now. That garrison can't be too far off."

CHAPTER 14

Not much time. The phrase echoed in Jerry's mind. So little time that the Chinese hadn't thought it necessary to tie them up. They were confident that he and Malloy could not possibly escape and survive a freezing night at this altitude. And any moment the two soldiers might return with more guards and an interpreter.

He tried to recall what he had read about interrogation of American prisoners in Korea. Solitary confinement. Fake confessions. Brainwashing. "What was it like, Tom?" For the first time he used Malloy's Christian name. "The questioning, I mean."

"It wasn't good. Whatever they say, don't sign anything.

Just tell them your name, occupation student, hometown. That's all."

"Did they use—torture?"

"No. Think about something else."

Maybe, he thought, Ang Nuri had witnessed their capture from a distance, and would report it to John Conrad. But what could Conrad and Rick and a few Sherpas do against Chinese troops? Nothing. And it would take many days for the news to reach the nearest American official in Katmandu. By then they might be hundreds or thousands of miles behind the Bamboo Curtain.

If they were ever going to escape, the time was now. Without help. On their own. But how? As Malloy had said, they could not overpower two alert, armed men.

The air was close and stuffy and he had become painfully conscious of his thirst, watching the Chinese consume quantities of hot unsweetened tea. He was tempted to ask for a drink. His gaze strayed over the hut and came to rest on their two packs. "Tom," he said, trying to keep his voice matter-of-fact, "didn't you bring along a supply of that knockout drug?"

"Sure. The kit's in my pack. Why?"

"If it worked on Big Red it ought to work on a man."

"It wouldn't take as much to knock out a man. But those two aren't going to sit still while I mix up a solution and load the rifle."

"Not that way."

Hurriedly Jerry outlined his scheme. Malloy scratched his head and a gleam came into his eyes. "It's supposed to be shot directly into the blood stream, but I don't see why it wouldn't absorb through the stomach wall. Take longer, of course."

"What if they taste the stuff?"

"That's a chance we'll have to take. But Chinese Army tea is bitter as witches' brew, very strong."

"Tell me when you're ready."

"I'll try to make it look good," Malloy said. "Here goes."

The two Chinese had been talking in low tones and both looked up when he began to cough. Sputtering and choking, Malloy slumped to the floor. The performance was so convincing that Jerry, if he hadn't known, would have thought Malloy was having a fit. He rolled and groaned realistically and clutched both hands to his stomach. The officer jumped up in alarm.

"He's sick," Jerry cried. He pointed to a pack, then to the fire and made the sign for drinking. "Medicine."

The officer scowled suspiciously and bent over Malloy, who went into another coughing spasm. Jerry pointed again and finally the officer relented. He picked the pack off the floor and handed it to him, and motioned toward the pot.

Trying to hide his nervousness, Jerry pulled out the bottle and unscrewed the top. Both Chinese, he observed from the corner of his eye, were intent on Malloy who, by holding his breath, had made his face turn purple. Advancing to the fire, he turned his back to them, dipped out a bowl of tea and emptied the whole bottle of drug into the pot. For a second he watched it dissolve in the dark simmering liquid, then turned back to Malloy.

On his knees, he poured some tea down Malloy's throat and gradually the convulsions subsided. In another minute or two Malloy's "attack" was over. He sat up and blinked weakly and smiled his gratitude at the Chinese. They shrugged and backed away and resumed their low-voiced conversation.

Jerry held up two fingers in a vee. Malloy gave him a bare wink and closed his eyes.

For a long while the Chinese went on talking. The air was so foul with smoke that Jerry had difficulty breathing. It stung his eyes and nostrils and he fought off the tickle in his throat. If he started coughing now they would surely get suspicious. Then the soldier pumped at his bellows to revive the fire and dipped out another bowl of tea which he handed to the officer.

Jerry felt Malloy tense beside him. The officer took one sip, made a face, sniffed at his bowl, and said something to the soldier. The soldier stirred the pot with his finger, dipped out a second bowl, and sampled it. With much smacking of lips he drank the contents down. The officer emptied his bowl on the floor and refilled it from the pot. Between swallows he lighted a cigarette, sipping leisurely.

Jerry tried not to stare. He had dumped enough drug into the pot to knock out a pair of elephants. But would it work like this? If so, how soon? Four minutes? Ten? An hour? He began to count.

A puff of wind swooped down the smokehole, scattering ashes and embers from the fire. The hide door flapped and fell back into place. Jerry's nails dug into his palms. The moan of the wind sounded like human voices. The officer peered outside, glanced at his wrist watch impatiently, and finished the last of his tea.

The soldier was the first to show signs of discomfort. Sweat beaded his forehead and he fumbled with the button at his collar. He mopped his face and leaned against the wall. Watching him through narrowed eyes, the officer spoke sharply. The soldier grunted an answer. Then the rifle slipped from his hand and clattered on the floor. He bent to retrieve it and fell forward on his face like a limp doll.

The officer shouted at him, and prodded his ribs with a boot. Then, as the realization dawned that he'd been tricked, he suddenly swung around on Jerry and Malloy. His eyes were murderous as he raised the pistol. It wavered in his hand. Staring into the muzzle, Jerry felt his skin crawl. The officer screamed at them in Chinese, his face livid with rage.

Then a glassy look came over his eyes. His arm fell, as though he were too weary to hold it out. He squeezed the trigger, the pistol cracked, but the bullet plowed harmlessly into the dirt at his feet. He tried to fire again but the effort was too much for him. His knees buckled and he fell across the prostrate soldier.

Malloy leaped to his feet and grabbed the pistol from his hand. Kneeling down, he put an ear to the man's chest. "Out cold," he said. "But I don't know for how long. Let's move!"

Jerry needed no prompting. They struggled into their jackets, pulled on their gloves, and shouldered their packs. Malloy smashed the Chinese rifle against a rock. "Leave the radio. We'll have to travel light."

Jerry took one last look around the hut. Here was warmth

and shelter and food of sorts. But not for them. "That officer'll catch it for letting us escape."

"We haven't made it yet," Malloy said.

The wind hit them like a body blow as they stepped through the doorway. The sky was clear with no moon, a factor in their favor, but the temperature must be close to zero, Jerry thought. There would be no stopping along the way for sleep. A man could freeze to death in minutes if his circulation slowed to the critical level.

They peered up and down but the canyon seemed devoid of life and sound. Malloy took the lead climbing up the steep trail by which they had descended, and the faint glow from the smokehole dwindled in the darkness below. They toiled up through the rocks and at the top paused to draw air into their tortured lungs. Suddenly Malloy gripped Jerry's arm.

The hut's squat silhouette was barely discernible far beneath them. Around it milled a swarm of antlike figures, ten or fifteen, too many to count accurately at a distance. The clink of metal carried on the wind. More soldiers. Guns. A yell floated up from the canyon bottom and the figures exploded into activity.

"Troops from the garrison," Malloy whispered.

Jerry shivered. They had made their getaway just in time. Even so, they had only a bare start, perhaps fifteen minutes, with miles yet to travel.

"Hit the trail, boy. We'll give 'em a run for their money."

With the wind at their backs they turned into the south. By starlight they followed the footprints they had made across the plateau the previous afternoon. Fortunately the snow crust was so hard that they left no fresh tracks which their pursuers could follow. They plodded along mechanically, alternating the lead. They seldom spoke. There was no sign of pursuit but they knew the Chinese would make a supreme effort to recapture them. It was like a deadly game of hare-and-hounds, Jerry thought. As a last resort the Chinese would shoot.

Shortly before dawn they came to a patch of loose broken rock and Malloy called a halt. "We'll hole up here," he said. "May not find anything better."

"Why not keep going?"

"Come daylight we'll stand out against the snow in these dark clothes. They can see us for miles. And once the snow softens they'll pick up our tracks. Maybe this way we can fox 'em."

Some distance up on a rocky hogback, which commanded a wide sweep of countryside, they scooped out a shallow pocket and bellied down. It was something he had learned as a GI in Korea, Malloy explained: when you don't have camouflage, take advantage of the natural terrain.

Lying motionless, Jerry felt the bitter cold bite into him. It seemed senseless to throw away their lead, but he followed Malloy's example and waited. Before long half a dozen shadowy shapes flitted by on the trail below, as silent as wolves. They were wearing snowshoes and they passed quickly from sight across the frozen gray landscape.

"Snowshoes," Malloy said. "They can cover a lot of territory in a day on those."

"They may bump into Rick and Conrad."

"I doubt it. They'll double back this way once they figure out we're behind them. Our best bet is to lie doggo."

Gradually the night faded and a rosy flush spread over the eastern sky, outlining the cone of Kang Peak to the south. Under the sun's rays the rocks began to warm up and the fierce glare off the snow struck wickedly at their eyes. Jerry slipped on his dark goggles, but Malloy hunted through his pockets without success.

"Must have dropped them in the hut," he said.

They looked at each other in dismay. "We can trade off with mine," Jerry offered.

"No, you need them. Thanks anyway." Malloy folded his handkerchief into a pad and bound it around his head and pulled his hat down over his eyes. "Not exactly lightproof but it helps."

They ate a candy bar apiece and melted snow in a plastic cup and mixed up the last of their lemon juice concentrate. Jerry was still hungry and thirsty and so tired he could hardly hold his eyes open. But someone had to be on lookout. The sun beat down with surprising heat, reflected off the snow.

"If anything happens," Malloy said, "that we shouldn't get back, I want to tell you this, Jerry. You're going to be a top-notch naturalist some day."

"You think so?"

"I've seen a lot of youngsters come and go in my classes. You'll get there. Believe in yourself. Work. You can be an-other Carl Sebold."

"How about another Tom Malloy?"

"Don't make the mistakes I've made. It never pays to hurry

and cut corners in any kind of scientific research. That's one lesson I hope you've learned from me."

"Sure." He realized this was an apology, that Malloy was trying to make up for all his months of criticism and fault-finding.

"And while I'm on my soapbox," Malloy went on, "don't ever get cocky. No matter how good you are, there's always someone a little better or smarter. We all need some of that old-fashioned virtue called humility. End of lecture."

"What would you do if that yeti walked right in front of us now?"

Malloy smiled. "Trick question. Well, I wouldn't budge out of this hole. I've discovered there are more important things in life, believe it or not, than catching a yeti."

Despite his good intentions Jerry dozed off. He fought it. He pinched himself and rubbed his face with snow. But his eyelids came down like leaden weights. He drifted off into a deep, exhausted sleep. When he awoke much later the sun was high in the western quarters. He had been asleep for hours.

With a stab of guilt he saw that Malloy had removed the bandage from his eyes and was scanning the horizon. Malloy had taken over the lookout duty while he slept. "Tom, your eyes! Why didn't you wake me?"

"You'd have slept through a typhoon. Look, I think we're due for a return visit."

Several dark specks had appeared on the distant skyline. As they approached they materialized into six Chinese soldiers, the sun glinting on their rifles. Their advance was slow and methodical, not single file now, but in a spread formation.

"They know. Trying to pick up our trail."

Minutes later another squad of soldiers snowshoed over the rise and joined the others. They gathered in a little knot, apparently for further orders, then spread out again at intervals of about thirty yards and resumed their advance. Now and then an officer, in the center of the oncoming line, blew on a whistle and signaled his men by hand.

When they reached the base of the rockfield, two soldiers unfastened their webs and climbed up toward the hogback. Jerry flattened in the hollow. The whistle shrilled again and he could hear the crunch of boots on rock, drawing steadily closer. Through a crack he saw the head and shoulders of the first soldier. The Chinese stopped a few feet away, shaded his eye against the sun, peered around, and walked on.

The footsteps receded. One soldier called to the other and laughed. On the far side of the rocks they sat down, put on their showshoes again, and hurried to overtake their comrades. Whistles and voices faded as the patrol dwindled across the plateau to the north.

Limp with relief, Jerry stared after them. "The sun was in his eyes," he said. "That soldier looked straight at me."

"How many were there?"

"Twelve." He looked around at Malloy's swollen, inflamed eyes. "Can't you see?"

"Not much. That sun caught up with me." Malloy tied the bandage around his head. "My own fool fault, losing those glasses."

"Maybe you'll be all right once the sun goes down."

"I can't tell light from dark. This snow blindness takes a couple of days to wear off sometimes."

"Two days! But we—"

"We're in a jam, Jerry. You'll have to be my eyes."

The next few hours were the longest Jerry had ever known. As the sun sank behind the mountains the cold increased. Malloy cupped his hands to his eyes in agony. Because the soldiers might return at any time, they dared not leave the sanctuary of the rocks until it was fully dark. Their food was gone. In terms of distance they were at least ten miles from camp. In terms of time, leading a helpless, temporarily blinded man across the snow, Jerry could not guess.

When the last gleam of light had faded from the sky, he stood up and helped Malloy to his feet. "Any better now?" he asked.

Malloy turned his face up to the night. "Black. Everything is black. Can't even see my hand."

"Then I'd better carry you down over these rocks. You could trip and break a leg."

He got Malloy piggyback, bowing under the weight, and started down toward the nearest snow. It was perhaps a hundred yards, but it seemed more like a mile. He moved a step at a time over the loose jagged rocks, picking his way with infinite care. A slip and a fall here could injure them both. When he finally staggered out onto the level snowpack and put Malloy down, he was so drained of strength he collapsed on his knees.

"We'll never make it," Malloy said. "You go on alone."

"And leave you here?"

"I'll lie up in the rocks. Send the Sherpas back for me."

"You'd be frozen solid by morning."

He tied a short length of rope from his wrist to Malloy's wrist, took his bearings from the peak, and they moved on in tandem. At times he followed their old trail. In places he turned aside in an effort to find a smoother surface. They left the plateau behind and climbed down into the valley where he had first seen the yeti tracks. Occasionally, where the footing was dangerously rough, he carried Malloy on his back for short distances.

Then they began to fall. After the first few spills, Jerry lost count. Malloy took the brunt of the punishment, stumbling over hummocks or buried rocks and pulling Jerry with him. They slammed down on the frozen snow, picked themselves up, and limped on. A cut opened over Malloy's eye and Jerry gashed his knee. A single thought spun through his mind like a refrain: *keep going*. If he once stopped he could not will himself to move another foot.

And then it was light again, full day. Dawn had come without his being aware of the change. The glare struck at them and the snow turned soft under their boots. Reeling with exhaustion, Jerry stared down the next slope and pulled up short, and Malloy bumped him from behind.

"What is it?"

He pointed, forgetting Malloy couldn't see. A line of figures was climbing toward them. "Soldiers. They've spotted us."

"Chinese soldiers? Are you sure?"

One of the figures waved his hat and yelled.

Suddenly he wanted to hug Tom Malloy, laugh and cry at the same time. It was Rick, Rick and the Sherpas coming to find them.

CHAPTER 15

THE finale of Operation Kang left its mark on Tom Malloy. He was quiet and thoughtful and subdued in manner. He seemed a different man.

The Sherpas improvised a litter and carried him down to advance camp. By the next morning, after a rest and first-aid treatment of his eyes, he could see well enough to travel again. They started off for Terang immediately, anxious to avoid any more encounters with the Chinese.

From Rick, Jerry learned what had happened during their absence. Alarmed by Ang's report, the remaining members of the team had spent one day in a futile search. They had lost the trail, hunted until nightfall, returned to camp, and set off once more at daybreak.

174

"We thought you and Malloy had had an accident," Rick told him. "Maybe fallen in a crevasse. I couldn't believe that you'd run into Chinese troops. That Ang must own a crystal ball."

"Next time I'll listen to him," Jerry said. "For a while we had a one-way ticket to nowhere."

"I'm beginning to think you're a human lightning rod, my friend. Wherever you go, trouble strikes."

"The old jinx?" Jerry laughed and shook his head. "I'll never gripe about my luck again. And Rick, tear up that letter. We were dead wrong about Tom Malloy. He's no saboteur."

"*I* was wrong, you mean. Well, that leaves twenty-three suspects. I wonder if we'll ever catch the critter."

Three days later they reached base camp and received a rousing welcome. Because of the storm everyone had worried about them. Jerry and Malloy sat up most of the night retelling their story. Dr. Sebold had gotten back safely and was now recovered, as were Lars Johansen and the doctor. The expedition was reunited and, for the first time in weeks, at full physical strength. It was an occasion to celebrate.

But their valley had changed. Snow mantled the lower slopes. No more flowers bloomed in the meadow and the grass was turning brown. Nights were colder and noticeably longer. The herders had driven their yaks down from higher pastures. The season grew late.

With a long face Dr. Sebold announced his decision. Much scientific work remained to be done at camp. There were specimens to prepare and classify, field notes to record, final reports to write and evaluate. With so little time left and the weather so uncertain, he considered it unwise to send out another search team. They had failed on their number-one project, the yeti, but they had done their best. In one week they would leave Terang and start back for Katmandu.

The search for the abominable snowman had come to an end.

They heard the news in silence. Then Malloy cleared his throat. "Before we leave," he said, "I want to get this off my chest. If you ever head another expedition, Carl, I hope I'll be lucky enough to go along. It's been a privilege to work under you."

Dr. Sebold colored.

"One more thing, then I'll shut up. I've sounded off about what a mistake it was to bring a college kid on this expedition. Then I got to know Jerry Dunham. It's a pleasure to eat my words."

The next morning Jerry and Rick climbed to the village. Their first errand was to pay a farewell visit to the abbot of Terang Gompa. The old man received them in the lamasery, thanked them for their gift of tea, and asked about the expedition.

"He says," Rick translated, "he is happy that the missing yeti skin has been found."

Jerry blinked. "How does he know?"

"He says he can read it in your eyes. Good fortune will smile upon you now."

Jerry stared into the wise old eyes, deep-set in the ancient face. He would never understand how this holy man could know about an event that had happened months ago, thousands of miles away. But he had come to accept such mysteries. They belonged to these people and to their mountains.

The second errand was to inquire how many bearers might be available for the return journey. The *shikar* promised to do what he could. He was sorry to report that the village hunters had found no further trace of Big Red. By now the bear undoubtedly had left the glacier and returned to the high country, perhaps to Tibet.

They paid over the one-hundred-rupee reward and left. "I don't feel so badly about it anymore," Jerry said. "In a way I'm glad."

"Glad about what?"

"That Big Red got away. He belongs here. Somehow I hate to think of him shut up in a cage."

"You wouldn't have said that a few months ago. You've changed."

Had he changed, Jerry wondered. He didn't think so. But he saw certain things in a different light.

That afternoon the *shikar* paid a return visit, accompanied by three of the village elders. They bore an invitation to the *sahibs* and all their men. The village was giving a party for the expedition that night. There would be feasting and singing and dancing, and gifts for their American friends. Everyone was invited.

The people of Terang, the *shikar* said, hoped the Americans would return next year. They were always welcome. And one day perhaps they would capture a yeti.

On behalf of the expedition Dr. Sebold made a speech of acceptance. They were honored by such hospitality, he declared. In their hearts they would carry away fond memories of Terang.

After the villagers departed the camp buzzed with preparations. Men shaved and trimmed each other's hair, hurriedly washed dirty shirts, and dug wrinkled coats out of their duffels. The Sherpas and Nepalis were no less busy, cleaning boots and mending torn clothes. Everyone wanted to look his best for the gala affair.

The idea struck Jerry late in the afternoon. By dark camp would be deserted. Not a man would stay behind and miss the fun. This could be his last chance, his only chance.

He found Ross Howe in his tent and asked to borrow the tape recorder for a few hours, explaining that he wanted to record some bird calls. It was a light compact unit, powered by batteries, and he carried it over into the trees, well beyond earshot of camp, and switched on the mike.

Night after night he had listened to the voice of the news broadcaster. He knew every inflection and turn of phrase by rote. But it was not so easy to duplicate that clipped British tone. He tried several times, erasing one effort after another off the tape, before he produced a fair imitation.

Hurrying back to his tent, he set up the recorder and stared at the illuminated dial of his watch. The timing had to be exactly right, the same hour every night. Darkness was closing over the valley and outside his tent men were gathering for the party. Sudden doubt assailed him. What a harebrained scheme this was! It would never fool the wily Mr. X.

His second hand swept around to the numeral 12. He switched on the set, turned the volume up full, the spools whirred and a voice—his voice—boomed out across the dusk.

This is Radio Delhi. And now, the news in English. Government sources in Katmandu revealed today that a member of the Chinese Embassy staff has defected and asked for political asylum. Informed circles report that this person has turned over to authorities a complete list of Communist secret agents in Nepal. Arrests are under way with more expected hourly. This sensational—

A wild squawk of static drowned out the rest. Jerry snapped off the recorder. His "broadcast" had sounded crude and fake. But now that he'd started he had to see it through.

Rick poked his head through the tent fly. "What's this stuff about secret agents?"

"Too much interference tonight. I'll tune in tomorrow. Come on, we'll be late for the party."

A few heads turned curiously in his direction as he stepped out. Surely every man in camp had heard the recording. But only one should feel any apprehension. Either that, or somebody was laughing to himself at such a clumsy, transparent trick. One out of twenty-three. Their faces told him nothing.

In a gay, noisy group they crossed the meadow, all looking forward to an evening of relaxation. They passed the yak enclosure and came to the foot of the cliff, where they straggled into single file to climb the narrow village trail. Jerry hung back and fell to the rear. After a few steps he ducked behind a rock and waited until the last man disappeared into the darkness above. Then he hurried back to camp alone.

The row of tents looked ghostly in the night. He listened to the mutter of the creek and crept behind the empty bear cage, where he could watch the entrance to his own tent. Prepared for a long, cold vigil, he gripped the flashlight in his pocket. Only one fact he could be sure of: the saboteur understood English. But would he come tonight to smash the radio again? Or did he feel safe now?

As Jerry crouched there he tried to visualize the unknown Mr. X. As a saboteur he had not been very successful. He had dealt the expedition no crippling blows. He had been more of a nuisance, as though his heart was not in his work. A sort of Reluctant Red Dragon.

Half an hour passed. Sounds of merriment floated down from the village, laughter and snatches of music. Distant lanterns flickered like fireflies. In that crowd his absence would go unnoticed. Out in the meadow insects hummed their strident chorus and a bird croaked sleepily from the trees.

Jerry stiffened. A stone had rattled somewhere along the path. He slid the flash from his pocket and waited, silent and tense. Nothing moved that he could see. Then he heard a soft, rustling sound that might have been a footfall in the grass, animal or human. He leaned forward, straining to pierce the darkness. Another step. Then silence again.

As if by sorcery a shadow appeared beside his tent. A shapeless, faceless shadow that moved stealthily, ever so warily. It reached for the flap. His hand quaking, Jerry snapped on the light.

The beam caught a squat dark figure in its yellow cone. The man froze in place and a shudder wracked his frame. His back to the light, he covered his face with his fingers.

"Turn around! You can't run this time."

The man sagged, as though all resolution had melted from him. Slowly he turned. Light winked on a gold tooth.

It was Ang Nuri, the Sherpa from Sikkim.

"Young *sahib*, is you?"

"It's me, Ang." He felt no elation, only wonder and a kind of sadness. "Why, Ang? Why did you do it?"

The brown face screwed up. "Is mistake. I—I—"

"Don't lie, Ang. You came to smash the radio. You were afraid the next broadcast might give you away."

"Please, young *sahib*—" Tears spilled from his eyes and then he was weeping like a child.

Much later, after Dr. Sebold and Rick had returned from the village, they got at the truth.

Many months ago, Ang related, his father had made a holy pilgrimage across the frontier to a lamasery in Tibet. While there he had been seized as a hostage by the Chinese. An agent then had approached Ang and promised the old man would be freed if Ang "cooperated." He was to sign on with the next American expedition in Nepal and make sure that it failed, so America would lose much face among the local people.

At first Ang had refused, but the Communists applied more pressure. They brought messages from his father begging for help. His father would die, they said. So at last, because all Sherpas have great filial devotion, Ang gave in to their threats. He had to save his father, whatever the cost to his honor.

"Do you believe him?"

"I do," Dr. Sebold said. "Remember that Tibetan boy and his grandfather? They nearly died trying to escape."

Jerry nodded. He had the prayer board still. And he remembered something else: the day he had fallen on the ice and Ang had climbed down to rescue him.

"He admits everything," Rick went on. "He threw the rifle in the creek; he let Big Red out, broke the radio."

"Did he jimmy the brakes on the truck?"

"No, a Red agent in the crowd at Phari that night did it. You see, Ang couldn't land a job with us. We had our full Sherpa team. So they had to get rid of Kamin, or somebody. They didn't care if they killed him and you too, Jerry. But it had to look like an accident so we wouldn't be suspicious."

"I'm glad. I could forgive him all the rest, but not that."

It was an ugly, twisted story. But he looked at Ang's bowed head with more pity than anger. Only a simple man would have done what Ang did. *And what would you do,* Jerry asked himself, *if your father were a prisoner of the enemy? Would you turn your back or try to save him, however wrongly?*

"What happens to him now, Rick, by Nepalese law?"

"He'll be sent to prison."

"Dr. Sebold—" Jerry drew a deep breath. "Can't we let him go?"

"Let him go! This man is a confessed—"

"I know he is, sir. But he can't do us any more harm, not that he ever did much."

Dr. Sebold sighed and pinched his lip and glanced at Rick. "I think Jerry's right," Rick said.

After a long silence the director said sternly, "Ang, look at me."

Ang looked up fearfully.

"Ang, you've brought disgrace on yourself and on your people. But I'm willing to give you a chance, thanks to these two young fellows, who seem to have faith in you. Go back to your home in Sikkim. Tell the authorities about your father. Maybe they can get him released." Dr. Sebold's voice softened. "Now clear out of here."

Ang's face lighted up. "Oh, young *sahibs*, thank you! Ang Nuri thank you."

"Go on. Off with you."

Ang got to his feet. Head erect, he threw back his shoulders. Then he marched out of the tent into the night.

For some while after he had gone they sat without speaking and the sounds of revelry drifted down from the village. "My friends," Rick said and grinned. "My good Yankee friends, the Communists would call you soft."

"Maybe we are."

"No, it is not a weakness to be kind. It is a strength they do not understand. Perhaps someday you can teach them, as you taught Ang Nuri tonight. But in the end surely you will win."

It was the last day. All the extra porters had arrived. The packs stood ready. Tomorrow they would strike their tents, lash up the remaining gear, and hit the trail for Katmandu. Men went about their final chores with an air of anticipation, eager to start. Within a few weeks most of them would be home.

Jerry slung his camera strap over one shoulder and walked up alongside the creek. The water was low and he crossed easily from rock to rock. While the sun was still high he wanted to photograph another view or two. The valley, which

had been so strange and foreign to him once, was home now—
for one more night. It was hard to realize that his real home
lay half a world away.

He would be late registering at State when he got back,
which meant a load of classwork and labs and make-up exams.
He'd have to get a job, maybe at the taxidermy shop. A new
roommate at the dorm. All too soon the familiar routine would
close around him.

He found a place to his liking, took a meter reading, and
snapped half a dozen pictures, more than he had intended. It
was too late to return for another roll of film so he climbed
on leisurely, enjoying the solitude. He picked his way over
the moraine to the base of the glacier and turned up a side
trail that led to a point just at snowline.

The point commanded a sweeping panorama of peaks and
he stopped to admire the scene. Below him spread the valley,
dotted with tents, and across the way the stone buildings and
golden *chorten* of Terang Gompa glistened in the sun. He
would never see this sight again, he knew, nor the friends he
had made here: the lama, the hunter, the yak herder, the woodcutter. But each would evoke a special memory.

And then, as he glanced down, he saw in the snow at his
feet a single print. He sucked in his breath.

It was fresh, made perhaps that very day. Perhaps he, Jerry
Dunham, had frightened the animal away just a moment before, and only a mile or so from camp. The creature, the yeti,
whatever IT was, had made a bounding downhill leap and
touched one foot to the snow.

He looked around, up and down, in every direction, and

saw, as he had expected, nothing but rocks and smooth, unbroken snow. Should he call the others and launch another search? There wasn't time for that. He didn't even have a film in his camera. But what he did have, etched forever in his mind, was a picture of that perfect, unspoiled, solitary track.

To come so close and still to miss! Strangely, he felt no disappointment. Long ago Carl Sebold had said to him: "Don't guess. Get the facts first."

And Rick Dawa had said: "In this crazy world perhaps it is better to leave one little mystery unsolved."

Smiling to himself, he scuffed out the footprint with his boot and started down toward camp.

About the Author

Hal G. Evarts, who has traveled extensively in Asia, got his inspiration for this story about the yeti, the abominable snowman, from a Sherpa guide he once hired. The guide claimed to have actually been an Everest Tiger and spun some wondrous yarns.

A native of Kansas and a graduate of Stanford University, Mr. Evarts first worked as a journalist. He returned to the United States after active duty overseas during World War II and began writing fiction. His short stories have appeared in national magazines and a number of them have been adapted for television. *The Secret of the Himalayas* is his fifteenth novel, his third for young people. He writes mainly about foreign adventure and the American West.

Mr. Evarts lives in La Jolla, California with his wife and three children.